EDGE OF CONTROL

AN E.D.G.E. SECURITY NOVEL

TRISH LOYE

ACKNOWLEDGMENTS

This book is for my dear friends
Elena, Steena and Dara.
Without whom I wouldn't have had the courage to
publish. They are fabulous writing buddies as well as
staunch supporters. Thank you for showing me the way,
and for sharing a glass of wine (or butter shot) with me.

I'd also like to thank my sister Krista for her unfailing
support even when I made her read the unedited first
draft. Your enthusiasm carried me through this process.

And last but not least I want to thank my family.
My girls are the best distraction I could ever ask for.
(Yes, Georgia this story is for you and Scarlett.)
Patrick, my amazing husband, with his infinite patience,
is my sanity and my strength.
I love you all.

PROLOGUE

SOMEWHERE IN THE HINDU KUSH, AFGHANISTAN

Navy Lieutenant Jake "College" Harrison forced himself to lie still and reassess the situation. He wanted to curse and fire his FN SCAR into the Taliban lurking below, killing all the bastards he could see. But Jake had been a SEAL for nearly eight years, and he didn't let his emotions rule him. He'd learned that lesson long before joining the Navy. Once emotions came into play, judgment and reason went out the window, usually leaping to their deaths.

A soft curse came over his earpiece. "These aren't good odds, College." Petty Officer Second Class Rhys "Lucky" Lafayette was hiding among the scrub brush about fifty yards to Jake's left.

"Copy that, Lucky," Jake responded.

Jake surveyed the scene from his vantage point behind a grouping of boulders high above the village. The other two men in his team lay hidden along the ridge one hundred yards above him. The small village housed maybe two hundred Pashtuns, the warrior-like people native to this mountainous region of Afghanistan. His team's mission had been to meet with the elders and secure the village.

They'd already had two previous meetings. This was supposed to be a mere formality before the village elders decided to play host to a few members of the spec ops community until the fighting left the area. The village would gain protection, and the United States would gain another small foothold of eyes and ears in the Hindu Kush region.

The simple mission had gone completely SNAFU. Taliban soldiers swarmed the village below.

"What's your count, Scat?" Jake asked. Petty Officer Second Class Nick Scattalone had the sharpest eyes, and as their tech guru, he also had the best head for numbers.

"About twenty-five, College," he said. "It doesn't make sense. There's nothing around here for them."

"They could be transporting something," Rhys said.

"Or someone," Jake said. "Keep eyes on. I want to know who or what they're protecting."

"Roger that," the rest affirmed.

They all waited in their hides, occasionally ribbing each other, none of them breaking position. Jake remained silent.

"College, you having a nap over there?" Rhys asked after a bit.

Jake snorted, but didn't reply. He didn't have to. Rhys knew he wasn't asleep, since Jake wasn't the type to ever shirk his duties. Rhys had been with him through BUD/s—the Basic Underwater Demolition/SEAL training course—which, after surviving Hell Week together, made them closer than brothers. Now they served together on SEAL Team Five based out of Coronado and were sent anywhere in the world.

"Something's happening down there, College," Scat announced over their comms.

Jake focused on the village and the surrounding area. More Taliban came out of the trees. Two of them dragged a body between them. "Can anyone make out their prisoner?"

"Wait out," Scat said. "I'm changing scopes." A few seconds later they heard him swear. "It looks like it might be that journalist who got himself captured last week."

Dammit. "Well, that complicates things," Jake said. "Roddy, move to the ridge for a better signal and call this in."

"Copy that."

They wouldn't see Petty Officer Rodriguez moving upslope. All of them had trained extensively for covert ops like this one. Below them, a Taliban soldier hoisted the journalist upright. Jake could see him clearly through his own scope now. The journalist appeared to be barely conscious, leaning heavily on his captor. Another man walked up to the journalist and placed a pistol to his head, but he turned to the mountains, waving his other arm. He yelled something.

"I don't like this," Rhys said.

Jake wanted to curse, but he didn't. He forced an even, calm tone. "They know we're here."

"Would the village elders have told them we were coming?" Scat asked.

Four Taliban soldiers hauled two women and two children to the village's edge. Each held their weapon to a prisoner's head. Jake could see, if not hear, the wailing of the hostages.

"It looks like they did," Jake said. "We have high ground and can take out the shooters before they hit anyone."

"But won't the other tangos just turn on the villagers?" Scat asked.

"Not if we give them something to chase," Jake said.

Scat cursed softly. "But they might not fire."

"They're gonna fire," Jake said. "We all know it."

"Shit," Scat said. "We're all gonna be bloody heroes now."

"Or dead," Rhys said with a huff of laughter. "Come on now, Scat. College has never done us wrong yet. Trust him."

Jake ignored the banter. Some men needed to joke before battle. Instead, he focused on the Taliban fighter who held a young boy by the arm. Tears tracked the boy's cheeks, but he glared at the man. "I've got the asshole on the left with the boy. Rhys, take the tango with the other kid. Scat, you've got the two holding the women."

Scattalone carried an Mk 20 Sniper Support Rifle and was more than able to make the shots, even though he sat three hundred yards above Jake and six hundred yards from the village.

"What about the leader and the tango holding the journalist?" Rhys asked.

"I've got them," Jake said, thinking hard. Once the main players were taken out, it'd only leave about twenty Taliban against four heavily armed and superiorly trained SEALs. Without a doubt, they could do this. "Lucky," he said, "you take out any other asshole who tries to grab a hostage."

"Roger that."

"College?" Scat said. "What about our exfil?"

Their exfiltration plan had been to hump out of the valley the same way they'd come in. Probably not going to happen with angry Taliban on their tails and dragging a civilian.

"I'll grab the journalist and get him to the far ridge," Jake said. "It's easier than trying to get back up here with him. You guys haul ass and meet me there."

Rhys sighed over the line. "Dammit, College, you know I'm not letting you go alone. Are you sure about this? Is this guy worth getting killed over?"

"He's one of ours," Jake said. "We're not leaving him."

"Roger that," Rhys said. "Let's do it."

Jake and Rhys crept closer to the village, silently working their way between the rocks and stunted trees. As they did, the shouts of the Taliban leader grew more frenzied. Once they were within one hundred yards of the village, they both found places to take their shots from. Rhys lay prone about twenty-five yards from him, by a small boulder. Jake signaled him with his hand. Rhys responded the same way. They were ready.

"Roddy, you get a signal yet?" Jake whispered into his mic.

"Got it, College. Bird inbound. Extraction, ten minutes."

"They're close," Rhys said.

"Seems some other spec ops team was in the area hunting for this journalist. They want us to wait out," Roddy said.

The Taliban leader bellowed at the mountains and fired his pistol twice before swinging it back against the journalist's head. Jake knew enough Pashto to know the man was screaming for them to give themselves up.

As if. SEALs never surrendered.

The Taliban leader yelled to one of his men holding a woman. That man shoved her to her knees and held his AK-47 to the back of her head, execution style.

Fuck.

"No waiting. The hostages don't have time. We do this now," Jake said.

"Roger," came the replies.

"On my count. Three." He settled the butt of the FN SCAR into his shoulder and his cheek along the stock.

"Two."

He sighted on the tango holding the kid.

"One."

He breathed out.

"Fire."

Jake squeezed the trigger of his FN SCAR and took out the asshole. He swept slightly left with his rifle, sighted on the leader, and pulled the trigger again. Two down. He heard the echoing crack of his team's shots. All good.

"I'm going in," Jake said. "Cover me." His men would take out any Taliban that turned on him. He leapt up and sprinted toward the journalist, knowing Rhys wasn't far behind. He shot small bursts at the Taliban, concentrating his fire away from the villagers. Most of the Taliban hadn't even seen him yet.

The tango holding the journalist dropped him to the ground. Jake shot him as he sprinted toward the fallen man. The majority of the Taliban forces were just fanatics with guns. Most never had any kind of expert training, and for that he was thankful. But he still had to worry about all the stray bullets flying around.

He skidded to a stop by the unconscious journalist. The man had a slim build, which would make it slightly easier to run with him. Jake hauled him up by his arm, tucked his shoulder into the guy's waist, and pulled him into a fireman's carry. He held his FN SCAR up and turned to run.

A Taliban soldier stood grinning at him, his AK-47 pointed right at his gut. One of the village elders, a wiry, straight-backed old man, shoved a long knife into the Taliban soldier's neck. Jake ducked to the side as the dying man's AK-47 sprayed bullets. He nodded his thanks to the elder, who nodded back.

Time to go.

Jake switched out the mag on his FN SCAR and ran toward the closest trees. "Lucky?"

"On your six."

They sprinted into the trees while Rhys laughed maniacally.

"You are one crazy fucker," Jake told him as he shifted the weight of the journalist. The guy must have weighed about one-eighty.

"I'm in good company," Rhys said.

Jake wanted to keep up the banter, but couldn't. He concentrated on sprinting with his burden while running up a mountain. "Roddy," he panted. "ETA on the bird?"

"Three minutes," Rodriguez said. "The fuckers are giving chase. We're taking out who we can, but they're entering the trees. Haul ass."

"Wilco."

They ran. Jake ran straight up, only zigzagging around the trees, while Rhys paused every now and then to turn and fire at the enemy pursuing them.

"Move it, Jake. They're gaining," Rhys said.

Jake didn't bother replying. His thighs burned as he pushed himself harder than his body wanted.

One of the first things a SEAL learned was that the body didn't give up, only the mind did. He would make it to the top. They cleared the trees and he almost groaned at what he saw. Minimal cover. Some rocks and a few bushes, but basically a huge slope of scree-tiny chips of rock—where two steps up meant one back. They'd be slow-moving targets.

He pulled up. "Take him, Rhys. I'll stay here and hold them until you get up."

"I'm not leaving you behind," Rhys said, his Louisiana accent thick.

"You have to," Jake said, taking command. "Or we both die. Get this fucker up the slope and then cover me when I come. You've got one minute, Lafayette. Now move it."

Jake handed over the journalist and took a position higher up the slope behind a couple of large rocks. He tucked the butt of his FN SCAR into his shoulder and sighted through the scope. A Taliban soldier ran out of the trees, shooting wildly. Jake shot him, and the next one, and the next, keeping the enemy back and giving Rhys time to get the journalist to safety.

"Bird's coming in." Roddy said. "ETA one minute, College. Hold on."

"Roger that," Jake said. "Lucky, you at the top?"

"Almost. This fucker is heavy."

Jake continued to shoot. He noticed movement in the trees to his left. "They're trying to flank me. Scat, you in position? Do you have a visual?"

A scream from his left answered him. "In position," Scat said. "Tango down."

Jake breathed a sigh of relief. Roddy and Scat had made

it to his ridge and now waited at the top. He might just make it out of here.

"At the top, College," Rhys said. "Haul ass."

"Wilco." Jake did a last spray of bullets into the trees, switched out his mags, and sprinted up the slope to the ridge. He could see the outline of his three team members, their rifles pointed downslope toward him. The thumping of a helicopter sounded. It must be just on the other side of the ridge.

Puffs of dust and gravel bits rained around him from the Taliban soldiers' bullets hitting the scree. He zigzagged as much as possible while running upslope. He used his hands, scrambling over the rocks, desperate to make it to safety.

Something punched him in the thigh. He stumbled and slid back down the slope a few feet.

"Get up, Jake," Rhys ordered over the line.

"Moving," Jake panted, struggling to his feet. His left leg wasn't working properly, but he forced it forward, feeling wetness soaking his pant leg.

He stumbled again. Pain burned through his thigh, and screamed at him every time he put weight on it. He slowed, but kept going. He would not give up.

Then Rhys was there. And so was a large, dark-skinned guy in fatigues without an insignia. They grabbed him under the arms and half carried him the last steps.

"Who're you?" Jake panted even as pain gripped him.

"Let's do the meet and greet later," the guy said.

Six more men wearing the same unfamiliar fatigues shot their rifles downhill at the approaching Taliban. Rhys and the stranger took Jake toward a waiting helicopter, its rotor blades kicking up a dust storm.

A tall woman strode over to them, shouldering her rifle. Her helmet hid her hair, but her goggles were up, showing blazing blue eyes. "I'm Valkyrie, the team leader." She waved a hand at the dark-skinned soldier holding him up. "Doc's our medic, he'll see to your leg."

Rhys didn't move and the woman's face turned harsher than the mountains surrounding them. "Do you have a problem, sailor?"

She knew they were SEALs, even without identifying insignia.

"No, sir," Rhys said. "I mean, ma'am."

She rolled her eyes before facing Jake. "My team can handle this from here. Get on the bird."

Jake shook his head in confusion, pain making his thinking slow. "You're a woman."

Her voice hardened. "I'm a captain, and you're done here. This is now my mission."

"You're not spec ops." Jake's leg might be screaming at him, but no American woman was allowed in special operations.

"We're better than spec ops," she said. "We're E.D.G.E. operators. Now get your ass onboard."

She walked away.

"I think I'm in love," Rhys said, staring after her.

Jake turned to the soldier nicknamed Doc, determined to get answers even though his leg had started to shriek with pain. "Edge?"

"E.D.G.E.," he said, helping him to the waiting helicopter. "Elite Digital and Global Enforcement."

"Never heard of it," Jake said.

"That's the idea," the man said with a grin.

CHAPTER 1

ONE YEAR LATER...

The rhythmic slapping of Danielle Everett's running shoes on the paved walk accompanied her deep breathing. Only one more kilometer left in her run. She stretched her pace and pushed herself to go faster, pumping her arms. The path curved through the trees, out of sight.

A tall, dark-haired man stepped into view. She stumbled, her heart stuttering as adrenaline flooded her system. She started to slow when he turned and whistled. A golden retriever came racing to his side.

Her brain switched on and she began noticing details

about him. Not tall enough. And, as she jogged closer, not muscled enough, or good looking enough. Not him.

She was safe.

"Dani, you witch," her friend, Tassia, called out from behind her before huffing a laugh. "I give up. I'm walking the rest of the way."

Dani didn't reply, the adrenaline leaving her shaky. She poured on the speed, sprinting on her toes and pushing hard with her quads. Her breath came in short bursts. She passed the man and his dog, determinedly not looking at him as she followed the path in Parc du Mont-Royal. Tass wouldn't be able to see her through the trees, but Dani didn't stop or slow even a bit.

Tassia wouldn't get lost. Besides, even though it was early morning, lots of people were out enjoying the warm spring weather. Dani gained more speed, her long, dark ponytail swinging, tension thudding out of her with each footfall as the path lowered, coming down off the Mountain, the name Montreal natives gave the park because of its height and views of the city.

Dani couldn't slow down. She compulsively pushed herself. She always wanted to see if she could do just a little bit more, a little bit faster, a little bit better. Besides, she needed to stay in top shape, in case her past ever caught up with her.

The path opened up onto Avenue des Pins and she dodged pedestrians as she ran toward her apartment on Rue Sainte Famille. It still amazed her she'd lucked out with such a great neighbor, one who'd turned into not just a running partner, but someone Dani could trust. Not with all her secrets, of course, but enough to call her a friend—and, at twenty-six years old, Dani had precious few friends.

She slowed as she came up to the four-story building, automatically scanning the street. A woman in a suit strode toward her and a tall guy in shorts and a hoodie jogged across the street. She ignored the woman, but kept track of the man until he turned the corner.

She'd finished stretching by the time Tassia showed up, panting and grimacing. "Seriously, woman, you are the devil." She flopped onto the steps leading up to the glass doors of the building. "I'm taller than you, I should be able to at least keep up with you. Did you even break a sweat?"

"Come to my MMA gym," Dani said. "Those guys'll whip you into the best shape ever."

"I'll leave beating people up to you," she said. "Though I do love dropping by and admiring the view."

Dani chuckled as she gave her friend a hand up. "Come over for breakfast. I'll make eggs."

Tass frowned. "I'm not sure I have time. The Public Prosecutor's building a big case against a company in town and I'm behind on my end."

"There's always time for food," she said. There had been too many times in Dani's life when food had been scarce. She tried to never miss a meal now.

Tassia worked long hours as a lawyer for the Office of Public Prosecution, the Quebec version of the Crown

Attorney Office, and her boss was a bear of a woman. Dani, on the other hand, worked in the research department at E.D.G.E. International Security, a corporate security firm. She dug up info about potential clients or sites for the field operators, and she was always careful to do it legally.

E.D.G.E. had only hired her because of Charles Lachine, a retired cop who worked as a consultant of some kind for them. Out of respect for Chuck, she'd never been late or sick in the six months she'd worked at E.D.G.E.

She showered and dressed in one of her three secondhand suits. The cut of the suit was loose, but not too loose. Her dark hair went into a bun and she skipped makeup, since her green eyes already attracted too much attention. The whole effect made her look mousy and worn, someone most people didn't notice.

Just the way she wanted it.

She stood at the counter making breakfast and going over what she would say today to the CEO of E.D.G.E., Adam Knight.

He had agreed to give her an interview for a field operator position. It meant travel, but she knew she could handle network security better than anyone. She was perfect for the job.

She scooped eggs onto plates. Well, she was perfect as long as they ignored her past.

"Seriously?" Tassia said when she entered the apartment and came into the kitchen, her hair still damp from her shower. "When are you gonna let me take you shopping for clothing that actually fits you?"

Dani shrugged. She knew how dowdy she looked. "I'm more comfortable this way."

Tassia's eyes narrowed in speculation. She opened her mouth, but Dani beat her to it.

"We'll be late if we don't eat now."

They sat down to eggs scrambled with mushrooms and cheese. Fried mushrooms made everything taste better.

"So, tell me about this mysterious guy you're going out with tonight," Dani said, wanting to derail Tassia's argument about her appearance.

Tassia looked away. "You can't freak out."

Dani's radar went off. "Why would I freak?"

"His name is Vadim," she said.

Dani's gut clenched. "Like short for Vladimir?"

"No, just Vadim." She sighed. "Look, I didn't want to tell you anything because I know how you hate anything Russian."

"I don't hate anything Russian," she said. "I'm—" Dani took a breath. She couldn't believe she'd almost told her. "I'm not prejudiced."

"You never want to go to that cool Russian restaurant in the Village. And you avoid anyone with an Eastern European accent or name."

All true, but she wasn't prejudiced. She'd need to work harder at this. Dani sighed out her tension. "What's this guy's last name?"

Tass waved her fork at her, and her face got a stubborn

look. "Seriously, you don't have to worry. I may not know how to fight, but I can take care of myself."

Dani doubted that, but she only smiled and lightened her voice. "That's not what I meant. I'm just curious. Is he cute?"

She grinned. "Gorgeous."

Dani forced an answering smile. "So…his last name?"

Tassia pushed the eggs around on her plate with her fork. "I'm not sure I should tell you." Her lips pressed together. "Not after what you did last time. I like this guy, Dani. Just trust me."

"Please tell me he's not married," Dani said.

She frowned. "He's not married."

"Then what's his last name?"

"Fine. It's Levkov. Vadim Levkov." She stood up. "But you are not running a background check on him. You ran off the last guy I dated with your questions and 'concern.'" She finger quoted the last word.

"He was dating other women."

"I don't care. I'm a grown woman and I don't need you playing big brother."

"You mean big sister," Dani said lightly, but it was too late. She'd lost her. Tassia strode away and the front door clicked shut. Firmly.

"Case closed," she muttered.

E.D.G.E. INTERNATIONAL SECURITY:
WE GO TO THE EDGE
SO YOU DON'T HAVE TO.

Jake scowled at the sign on the wall before entering the large plush office in downtown Montreal, trying not to limp. His leg ached from sitting on a six-hour flight.

What the hell was he doing here? How had he gotten to this point? He cursed the mission that had gone so disastrously wrong a year ago. So wrong that even now, after a year of recovery and intensive rehab on his leg, the doctors wondered whether he could keep up with his SEAL team. He knew his men trusted him, but the higher-ups all shook their heads. His teeth ground as he remembered his CO asking—no, *telling* him—to take this interview and work with this company for the next two weeks as a trial.

The same company who'd rescued them from the Taliban twelve months ago. E.D.G.E. International Security. A cover for what they really were.

A damn merc company.

He hated mercenaries. They worked for the highest bidder, got in the way of real operations, and most of the ones he'd met had questionable morals.

How could his CO do this to him? To them?

He glanced sideways at Rhys. At least his buddy was with him, though he hated dragging him down the same freaking rabbit hole he'd been sent down. He'd never heard of a SEAL or any spec ops guy being sent to interview with a civilian company, let alone a company in another country.

They stood at ease in the empty office, waiting on some ex-SEAL who ran the show. It was only because the head honcho used to be a SEAL that he'd agreed to this. Once it was over, he and Rhys were hopping on the first flight to Coronado and back into training, bad leg or not. Their team was being deployed in a month. He'd prove to the brass that he could do the job.

"Do you think they're going to offer us a gazillion dollars? Maybe we'll get to protect supermodels," Rhys said. He stood to the side of the window looking out over the busy street below. Neither of them would ever stand in front of an open window again, no matter what country they were in.

"Won't matter," Jake said. "We do our two weeks, turn down the permanent position, and then we're out of here."

A door whisked open and a dark-skinned, fit man in his early forties walked in. His shaved head gleamed in the overhead light.

"Gentlemen," he said. "I'm Adam Knight. Your CO told me that you two might be interested in working with us."

Jake squared his shoulders. Better to cut this off now. "Actually, sir," he said with respect, "we're not interested in working for a mercenary company." Rhys gave a sharp nod of agreement.

Knight studied Jake. "I read the medical report on your leg. If you stay with the teams, chances are you'll end up behind a desk."

"Even so, sir." Jake shrugged. "It just doesn't sit right with me. Merc companies are either babysitters for people with too much money, or tend to do jobs that could interfere with real missions."

Knight walked over to his desk and flipped open a file. "One of the jobs we did last year saved a SEAL's life."

Jake shifted his feet. "It's the mercenary part I'm having a hard time with, sir. No offense."

Knight sat down. "No offense taken," he said, leaning back in his chair while a smile crept onto his face. "You've just confirmed that E.D.G.E.'s cover is fully in place, and I'm happy to let you know what we really do."

Jake frowned and shared a glance with Rhys. Was this guy for real? He decided to spell it out for him anyway. "Sir, we know E.D.G.E. isn't just a security company. That's why we're here, right? It's also a mercenary company and you want to hire us."

Knight's smile widened. "We're not a merc company, Lieutenant Harrison. That's our cover. E.D.G.E. is Elite Digital and Global Enforcement.

"This is a highly classified government-run unit. We have operators from all arms of both the United States and Canada's military, as well as the CIA and CSIS." He stopped smiling and placed both palms on his desk. "We are a unit that transcends boundaries. We're the one governments call when they can't get past the red tape or legal bullshit that interdepartmental desk jockeys insist on. We go in and get the job done."

Knight tapped the papers on his desk. "I've studied your files and would like to offer you both positions as operators at E.D.G.E. I have a small assignment being run here in Montreal that I'd like you both to sit in on. At the end of two weeks you can tell me how you feel about working with us."

Jake studied the man sitting behind the desk. His CO had told him to listen to Knight and to consider his offer carefully, because it would only come once.

He glanced at Rhys, who arched a brow and lifted one shoulder a fraction in a discreet shrug, clearly as surprised as he was.

"We've been ordered to work with you for the next two weeks, sir. We'll let you know our answer when our tour is done."

"Good enough," he said. "And gentlemen? Lose the uniforms while you're here."

Dani sat at her computer in the research department as she pulled up anything she could find on Vadim Levkov. Her desk and one other empty one faced a wall, her monitor visible to anyone who walked by. Four other work stations were arranged in a semicircle behind her, so only the research assistants working there could see their screens.

Dani disliked that she was left out of the inner sanctum of the research department, but she had bigger ambitions than sitting with them, so she tried not to let it bother her. She just made sure to tilt her monitor, so that anyone walking behind her would have to bend their head to see what she worked on.

As a major international security firm, E.D.G.E. had a huge database of public profiles, but she itched to dig deeper. She had the skills, she'd just promised not to use them.

The database turned up four Levkovs in the Montreal area, none of them lawyers, and none of them cute enough to make Tass do a happy dance. She bit her lip and her fingers hovered over the keys. She could dig deeper. Maybe hack into the DMV server.

She clenched her hands into fists and pushed back from her desk. No. She wouldn't break Chuck's trust. She'd just have to do this the old-fashioned way.

She'd follow Tass on her date.

Tass would kill her if she found out, but Dani knew how to blend. She was better at it than anyone could guess.

"If you don't have any work to do, I'm sure I can find you some."

Dani sighed as Ashley Thompson, otherwise known as the Bane of Dani's Existence, stopped in front of her desk.

Ashley dressed like a cross between a runway model and a librarian, her dark hair pinned up, her makeup flawless and her clothing tight, but not too revealing.

"I have work," Dani said, clicking onto a benign website about a potential future client. "And I sent you the information you requested already. Check your inbox."

"The report wasn't detailed enough," Ashley sniped. "As the official head of marketing, do I need to remind you to take this job seriously? That is, if you want to continue to work here."

Dani grit her teeth. "I take this job very seriously. And you're the *only* marketing employee, so I hardly think that qualifies you to be the head of a department."

Ashley huffed. "Just because you're Chuck's little pet doesn't mean you'll ever make it out of research. Unlike you, I'm going places with E.D.G.E. Soon, you'll be working for me." Her heels clicked as she strode back to her office.

Dani was still glaring after her when Chuck showed up. "Hey, kid." Even though he'd retired from the force five years ago, he still stood like a cop, feet planted and weight balanced, relaxed and yet attack-ready. His gray hair was military short and he hooked his hands in his belt. "You ready for this?"

Dani stood up. At five-foot-eight, she was almost eye to eye with Chuck. She lifted her chin. "Always."

They walked over to the elevators. E.D.G.E took up floors five, six, and seven of the building. Dani had only ever been on the fifth floor and had never even seen the company president. It had been the research department head that she'd interviewed with. She didn't think even he had access to floors six and seven.

"Now remember," Chuck said as they rode the elevator to the seventh floor. "This—"

"—is a long shot," she finished. "I know, Chuck, but I appreciate the chance. Hell, I appreciate having a real job."

His lips compressed. "I hope they can see your talents. It's a damn shame they're going to waste."

She waggled her eyebrows. "Maybe I'll win over the big guy with my sparkling personality." She laughed at his grim expression. "Seriously, Chuck, don't worry. I got this."

"That's what I'm worried about."

On that odd note, they left the elevator and strode toward the outer receptionist, who sat typing, a small earpiece half hidden by the chestnut hair falling to her shoulders. Her clothes were trim, but not tight or showy like Ashley's.

She looked up and smiled. "Hello, Chuck."

She gave the slightest pause as she saw Dani. "And you must be Danielle. Mr. Knight is in a meeting at the moment, please take a seat. Can I get you a coffee or tea?"

They shook their heads. Chuck eased into a chair while Dani moved about the room, trying to hide her restless energy. She pretended to inspect each piece of art, but couldn't have told anyone what she looked at.

She wanted this job. As much as she appreciated having a job with health benefits, research was not what she wanted to do. She needed more of a challenge.

A field operator in a network security company sounded like geek heaven to her.

The double doors leading to the inner sanctum opened. Mr. Knight, the founder and head of E.D.G.E., walked out with two other men, both dressed in dark blue Navy uniforms, rows of ribbons adorning the left breast of their jackets.

All three had muscled bodies and moved with the same grace as the top fighters in her gym. It was rumored Mr. Knight had once been a Navy SEAL, and seeing him now, she could believe it. With his fit physique and commanding presence, he radiated power, as did the two men beside him.

Tassia would be drooling over the guys in uniform, both taller than Dani, and both gorgeous. The blond one was a few inches taller than his friend and lean, like a swimmer. He pushed back shaggy blond hair from a movie-star-gorgeous face and grinned at her.

Dani nodded back cautiously. With those looks, he had *player* written all over him. She dismissed him and turned to the other man.

His hair was dark and crew-cut. It highlighted his hard jaw and almost sharp cheekbones. His heavily muscled body seemed to strain the seams of his jacket. This man wasn't classically good looking like his friend, but he was definitely all male. She drew in a breath.

The dark-haired man turned and his sharp gaze seared her. Her mind froze for an instant, as if she'd been pinned unexpectedly by a stronger opponent. Her heart beat faster and she could feel her cheeks redden. His gaze flicked to Chuck before returning to her, studying her. His eyebrows drew together slightly.

"And this, gentlemen," Mr. Knight said, waving Chuck

forward, "is someone I couldn't run my operation without: Charles Lachine, my police liaison. Chuck's a retired detective with the Montreal Police." He turned to the two men. "Chuck, this is Lieutenant Jake Harrison and Petty Officer Rhys Lafayette. I'm trying to lure them into taking positions as field operators with us."

The men all shook hands before Chuck waved a hand at her. "This is Danielle Everett from research, the computer expert I told you about."

Mr. Knight shook her hand. "Danielle, it's good to meet you. Your department head thinks highly of you, and Chuck has only glowing things to say."

She nodded. "Please call me Dani, and thank you, sir."

Lieutenant Jake held out his hand. "It's nice to meet you, Danielle."

His grip was strong but not overbearing, and his large hand encompassed hers, warm and rough. She suppressed a shiver. His pale eyes were actually gray.

Now was not the time to notice eyes.

She pulled her hand away and turned to the other man, though Jake still watched her.

The blond movie-star lookalike, Rhys, shot a quizzical look at Jake before he smiled and shook her hand. "A computer expert?" His easy drawl made her think of warm pecan pie and magnolia trees.

He was a charmer, and probably used his looks to his advantage. All good-looking men did. She'd had experience with men just like him. She smiled politely at him and nodded.

"A first-class hacker," Chuck stated, as though he'd trained her himself, though it had been the complete opposite.

Lieutenant Jake focused even more on her, as if he wanted to delve inside and discover all her secrets. "A hacker? You definitely don't fit the stereotype."

Warmth rushed to Dani's cheeks. "And what's that?"

His gaze traveled the length of her and something inside her tightened.

He squinted slightly as if trying not to smile. "That most hackers are rebellious teens with too many piercings."

Dani almost touched her belly button ring, but clenched her fingers into a fist instead. Jake's gaze focused there for a moment before he looked back at her face. "You're dressed very conservatively, as if you don't want people to notice you. But a hacker, by profession, seeks attention. You're an interesting dichotomy, Danielle."

Dani wasn't sure if that was a good thing or not. Her heart thudded in her chest and she couldn't look away from his intense eyes. "It's Dani."

Rhys interrupted their conversation. "Dani, it was nice to meet you, but we should get going." His smile was professional. Her heart rate eased back to normal.

She nodded and stepped back, refusing to look at Jake again.

"Please excuse me," Mr. Knight said to Dani and Chuck, "while I walk these gentlemen out."

She waited with Chuck, trying unsuccessfully to dismiss

those piercing gray eyes from her mind. She hadn't let a man affect her in years, and she certainly wasn't going to start now. Not when the job of a lifetime was on the line. She pushed Jake, his broad shoulders, and his gray eyes into a box in her mind and locked it tight.

When Knight returned, they followed him back into a large office with a view of the Montreal skyline. A wooden desk sat where it had a view of both the windows and door.

A leather couch and chairs took up one area of the room. A long conference table stood in front of the windows, with a piece of advanced hardware in the middle of it. It was a virtual touchscreen monitor, and she itched to play with it.

Mr. Knight steered them past the comfortable seating area and led them to his desk. He sat behind it and waved a hand at the chairs in front.

He opened a file folder on his desktop. Her employee picture was clipped inside, along with two sheets of paper. She couldn't read them, but she'd bet one was her pitifully short resume and the other some kind of work progress report. She hoped Ashley hadn't contributed to it.

"So, Dani, you're hoping to become one of our field operators." Mr. Knight leaned back in his chair and stared into her eyes. "I have to tell you that your chances are slim. We look for highly qualified individuals and your resume leaves a lot to be desired." He nodded at Chuck. "In fact, we only hired you for the research department because Chuck vouched for you."

"And I thank you both for that opportunity, sir, but I

do believe that my unique talents could be utilized to the benefit of the company."

Mr. Knight stroked his chin as he studied Dani. "There is no mention of unique talents in your resume. Chuck has filled me in a bit, but could you elaborate?"

She took a deep breath. It was time to go all in. "I believe I could be a great asset for your security company. You see, I'm not just a hacker, Mr. Knight, I'm also an expert thief."

CHAPTER 2

"Don't worry about it, Dani," Chuck said as they walked back to the elevators. "You may not be an operator, but you got a promotion. You're in IT now."

She tried to smile, but the lead ball in her stomach prevented more than a grimace. "I'm just doing more research and a bit of network design, not doing what I do best."

"You know, they'd trust you more if you trusted them."

Dani averted her gaze from his understanding one, shaking her head once. "I don't think they need all the sordid details of my past."

He paused. "They know Danielle Everett isn't your real name."

Dani still didn't look up. "So why don't they just fire me?"

Chuck waited her out.

She finally lifted her face and Chuck had a fatherly smile on his lined one. He'd always had her best interests at heart, acting almost like a parent to her. He really should have had kids of his own, but his wife had died young and Chuck had never remarried.

Dani figured that's why he'd taken such an interest in her when she was younger. They'd been two loners who'd found each other and declared themselves family.

Dani knew it was only because of Chuck that she had this job. Danielle Everett had only existed for five years, starting at age twenty-one. She should have forged a childhood when she'd created her new persona, then maybe she'd have the job she wanted.

Chuck slapped her on the shoulder. "They'll trust you eventually, whether they know your past or not. But remember, most of the field operators are military-trained specialists. You'll have to prove yourself."

She nodded, but didn't really agree with his assessment. How could she prove herself if they didn't give her a chance? Besides, who better to find security flaws in buildings than a former thief?

Unfortunately, Mr. Knight wanted her full background and wouldn't take her word for her abilities, even with Chuck vouching for her. She supposed she couldn't really blame him for his caution.

She left Chuck on the sixth floor, where he had a meeting

with the head of operations, and where her pass card didn't grant access. Only field operators and the CEO could access the sixth floor. She made her way back down to the fifth. She hardly ever saw field operators in the elevators, she realized. Either they worked odd hours, or they had a private one somewhere else.

She could look up the building plans. That wasn't illegal. She sighed. The thought of a puzzle usually distracted her, but the lead in her stomach stayed.

The elevator doors opened. Ashley stood near reception and Dani tensed. She really didn't want to speak with her right now. It had always struck her as odd that Ashley was the only person in marketing and sales, since the company managed quite a number of clients. Even so, Ashley never seemed to have that much to do and spent too much of her time trying to order around the research people. Dani hoped being in IT would at least get her farther from Ashley.

She scooted by her nemesis and started to pack up her desk for the move. No more complaining for her, she decided. This job was way better than waitressing, which was what she'd been doing six months ago.

Ashley waltzed over. "Have my dreams finally been answered and you've been fired?" she asked.

Dani didn't stop packing. She set her favorite mug with tiny computer code written all over it into a small box, along with a Mason jar full of pens. "I've been moved to IT."

"What?" Ashley's mouth dropped open. "No one told *me*."

Dani shrugged. "Mr. Knight just made the decision."

"You spoke with him?"

"I just came from his office."

"*His office?*"

"What's the big deal, Ashley?" Finished, Dani picked up her box and headed down the hall to the IT department.

Ashley followed her, sputtering. "No one sees Mr. Knight except the field operators."

Now that was odd. "Not even you?" Dani asked.

Ashley stopped walking, but Dani didn't. "Of course I see him, Danielle," she called after her. "I report to him directly and you'd better remember that."

Dani didn't bother answering. Ashley had just lied. How was it that someone in a position such as Ashley's never actually spoke with the CEO? The puzzle that was E.D.G.E. Securities just got a little more interesting.

She probably should be nicer to Ashley, in case she ever needed information from her. Dani snorted. That wasn't going to happen. She'd never been good at sucking up to people, especially people who liked to power-trip.

Jake Harrison had the air of someone in charge of others, but he didn't seem like the type to abuse his authority. She wondered what he did in the military—and why he was leaving it. You didn't get that kind of hardness in the body and especially in the eyes by doing anything easy.

He'd seemed to see right through her disguise. No one really looked past her blah suits and boring bun. No one noticed that she wore a type of armor, but he had. She wondered if he'd be interested in what was underneath her suit.

She shoved the thought aside. She had no time in her life for complications, and Lieutenant Jake Harrison wore *complication* like another medal pinned to his chest. Hopefully he wouldn't take the job with E.D.G.E.

Dani barely stopped her groan as she entered the IT department. The same size room as the research department, it held about ten desks with laptops, desktops, and the latest equipment. Her fingers itched to grab a keyboard and see what these servers held.

Most of the desks were occupied with intent men and women clicking keyboards. A few were people she'd never seen before. Operators, perhaps?

The cause of her almost-groan stood speaking with a tall Asian man in a *Doctor Who* t-shirt and faded jeans. Jake Harrison and his blond friend, Rhys, smiled and chatted with Mike, a guy from her MMA gym. Mike was a topnotch fighter, and his hard muscles showed people he wasn't just your typical geek. She'd known he worked here, but she'd assumed he was a field operator because she hardly ever ran into him.

All three men stopped talking and looked over at her. None of them spoke.

"I'm Dani from Research," she said to Mike. "I've been transferred to IT."

"Really?" Mike asked. "I didn't know you had the background."

Dani shrugged, her face warming. She bet he knew she hadn't gone past grade twelve. "I'm self-taught."

"Ah," Mike said. "Well, I'm the department supervisor. You can put your stuff down on that empty desk. I'll be with you in a minute."

He turned back to the men and Dani went to the desk indicated. Nearby was a reinforced metal door with deadbolts. It was the automatic-locking kind that needed a passkey to get through. She stared at the door a minute, wondering what could be behind it.

"Dani?"

She turned to Mike. Both Jake and Rhys still stood there. She shifted her feet, but smiled professionally. "Yes?"

"What's your area of specialty?"

She bit her lip, her eyes drawn to Jake, who'd arched an eyebrow in anticipation.

Mike's face fell a little when she didn't answer right away. "Do you have a specialty?" he prompted. "Networks? Building software? Hardware?"

"Hacking," Jake said, still watching her.

Mike's eyebrows rose. "Hacking? Are you any good?"

She pulled her gaze from Jake's. "The best. I'm a bit rusty, but Mr. Knight said you could probably use my skills."

Mike didn't say anything at first. She knew that the boxy suit she wore as camouflage didn't scream hacker, but she prayed he'd give her a chance. "I recognize you from the gym," he said finally.

Dani nodded.

"You've got good speed in the ring." Out of the corner of her eye she could see Jake's interest as he continued to study her.

"Okay," Mike said. "Let's see what you can do. Your computer isn't on the E.D.G.E. network. I want you to hack our system. Tell me when you get in." He turned back to Jake and Rhys and ushered them from the department, through the mysterious metal door. She couldn't see what was behind it, and none of them looked back.

She shook off the dismissal and sat down at her new desk. A smile bloomed on her face. She'd just been given permission to break into a secure server. Maybe this job wouldn't be so bad after all.

A little whoop of excitement left her when she finally cracked the network. She'd gotten into the main system hours ago, but had discovered a hidden network with multiple firewalls.

She stretched her arms over her head, cracking her back. Everyone else had gone home, but that didn't bother her. She'd also missed scoping out Tassia's date, but Tass was probably right and Dani needed to trust her friend's judgment. She'd quiz Tassia tomorrow morning before work and find out more about this Vadim. Besides, the puzzle of E.D.G.E. was too big for Dani to resist. She delved back into the information now open to her.

She skimmed the files she found. One marked Operations, one marked New Developments, the document titles inside both raised her eyebrows, but it was the personnel files she delved deeper into. She found the backgrounds on all the field operators.

She whistled as she scanned them. No wonder they had firewalls galore. The field operators didn't just have military training, most of them came from special operations. One woman was CIA and Dani recognized her from the gym. She kept skimming the info until Jake Harrison's file came up. It made sense E.D.G.E. had it, if he was applying to be an operator.

She bit her lip, but it took only a microsecond before she made her decision and clicked on it.

"A Navy SEAL," she murmured. She pulled up more of Lieutenant Jake Harrison's file, intrigued despite herself. He'd taken a lot of specialty training courses, like second and third languages, unarmed combat, jump master, and demolitions, but there was very little on what his operational duties had been.

Or to be more precise, there was information of past operations, but so much of it was classified and blacked out, she could barely read it.

She leaned back in her chair and took a breath. That trail was blocked and she was pretty sure the U.S. Navy wouldn't understand if she tried hacking their servers to satisfy her curiosity about a man she'd just met.

A thought had her tapping her fingers. Why would a

security company have such specialized personnel? She needed to see E.D.G.E.'s main operations. She started clicking on files.

The inner locked door burst open, slamming against the wall. Mike, with a pistol in hand, stood in front of her before she even realized who'd come through the door. His hard stare surveyed the room before focusing on her like an angry predator. He didn't lower his weapon, and neither did the two field operators following behind him.

"What the hell are you doing?" Mike asked.

Dani crossed her arms and lifted her chin, not wanting to show how freaked out she was by her supervisor pointing a gun at her. "Exactly what you asked me to do."

His eyes widened. "I didn't ask you to break into top-secret files. I asked you to infiltrate the network." He took a deep breath and released it, lowering his weapon and sliding it into a holster under his arm. He turned to the other two, a man with massive muscles and dark skin, and a petite brunette with eyes a lot colder than those depicted in her CIA photo.

"Call Knight and Blackwell. Give them a sitrep," Mike said.

"What should I say about her?" the woman asked in a monotone voice. She still hadn't put her weapon up, even though the big guy had.

Mike focused on her, but at least he had a small smile on his face. "Tell them the newest IT recruit set off the alarm. Nothing to worry about."

The female operator slid her pistol into a shoulder holster and opened the inner door again. Spiral stairs led up, most likely to the field operators' floor, but the door shut before Dani could see anything else.

"You set off an alarm," Mike said, "and we're very careful about our information. Some of the clients we deal with require…extreme precautions." He held her gaze and crossed his arms, placing his one hand very near the handle of his gun. "What did you find out?"

"Not much," she lied. Thank god she'd had a lot of practice. "I'd only just gotten in."

He studied her for a moment and then nodded. "Except for tripping an alarm, good work today. I'll see you tomorrow morning."

Dani shut down her computer, disappointed that she hadn't had a chance to more than glance at the operations file. She'd only seen a few country headings, ones like Iraq, Sudan, and Ukraine. Some of the world's major hotspots for conflicts at the moment. Maybe that's why the operators needed military backgrounds. She stood up to leave.

"Dani?" Mike said, waiting for her to look at him again. "Don't ever hack anything at E.D.G.E. again, or you're fired."

The next morning, Dani stopped by Tassia's apartment before heading to the gym. Her friend usually woke early, so Dani had no qualms about pounding on her door. Tass's date with the mysterious Vadim had already happened and she wanted details.

She also wanted Tassia's thoughts about what she'd found on E.D.G.E.'s computers—specifically, what kind of security company it was, and why it required highly trained armed guards in the middle of the night.

"Tassia?" she called. Why wasn't she up yet? It was unusual enough that she tried the door.

Unlocked.

She frowned as she opened it and called for her friend again. A peek down the apartment's short hall confirmed that Tass's bedroom door was open and a quick glance inside showed the usually mess of clothes, knickknacks, and magazines. Though it looked like she'd actually made an effort to clear off her work desk; it usually had piles of folders on it. Tassia must have already left for work and forgotten to lock her door again. She was going to have to give her another lecture on security.

Heels and a discarded cocktail dress lay on the floor by the bed. Clothes she'd tried on for her date?

Dani stilled, not sure what kept her in the doorway. Nothing was out of the ordinary. Tassia was probably at work, bursting with details about her date. Dani shrugged off her uneasiness.

She'd call Tass on the way to the gym.

CHAPTER 3

J ake parked his rental sedan in the MMA gym's underground parking lot. With his kit in a small duffel slung over his shoulder, he headed for the glass doors leading to the stairs.

The early morning air cooled his skin. He wore shorts and a t-shirt with a faded logo of a snarling seal holding both a bayonet and a pistol. The shorts exposed the puckered scar running down the side of his thigh, but he refused to hide it. At least he still had a leg to run with.

The gym was in a building two blocks from E.D.G.E. headquarters. A few of the other operators had mentioned it to him and Rhys as a good place to train. It occupied half of the second floor of yet another high-rise in downtown Montreal. Even with the other operators' recommendations, the wall of windows that greeted him made him wonder if this was just another frou-frou health club.

But past the small reception desk, he immediately approved of what he saw. This was no fancy club with spa treatments, smoothie bars, and aerobics classes. This was a gym he could feel at home in.

A full set of weights sat in one corner, with sparring mats in another. Heavy bags hung from the ceiling in another section, while a small stretching area lay just behind reception. This all surrounded a full-sized ring in the center of the room.

The smell of sweat, plastic mats, and disinfectant filled the air. Mostly men, though some women, boxed, jumped rope, wrestled, lifted, and hit bags. He saw more than a few of the operators he'd met yesterday. Rhys waved to him from the heavy bags.

Two people occupied the ring at the moment, both in sparring headgear, silky fight shorts, and hand wraps. A guy with muscles and tats fought a woman in a sports bra, her long dark braid hanging down her back. The woman's muscles gleamed with sweat, but it was her graceful movements that told of her experience in the ring.

This woman was a fighter. Her stomach rippled with muscles as she whipped her leg out in a roundhouse to the man's head. He leapt back, but she followed with a jab-cross combination that kept the man moving. Jake approved not just of her tactics, but of her smooth control. She was fast and fierce. Something about her compelled him and he moved closer to watch.

The man changed his stance and swept her latest kick aside, leaping at her with a powerful combination of punches and kicks. She blocked and evaded, never losing her calm control.

She deflected one brutal kick with her leg and spun into a back kick, catching the man in his stomach. He stumbled back. A coach on the far side of the ring called a halt.

"Jesus, Dani," the man said, rubbing his stomach. "What's up with you today?"

Dani? The dowdy computer hacker from E.D.G.E.?

The woman took off her headgear and confirmed his guess. "Sorry," she said. "I've got a lot on my mind."

She begged off a rematch and slid between the ropes, hopping to the ground in front of Jake. He sucked in a silent breath. He'd known she was more than she appeared, but who'd have thought such a body lived beneath the baggy suit? And why in the hell had she hidden it?

The woman obviously had a reason, and no matter how interesting a puzzle Dani posed, it was probably better for Jake just to let her keep hiding. Especially since he didn't plan on being here long.

She didn't move from where she'd landed, her gaze roaming over his chest and arms. His body heated as if she physically caressed him, and he caught her gaze with his. Her eyes widened and her lips parted. She wasn't immune to him and he smiled slightly at the thought, even as lust flashed through him.

A small, ridged scar, white with age, stood out near her shoulder. There was another on her stomach. They looked like knife wounds. He stepped closer, intrigued.

Who was this woman?

She moved back. "You want something?"

His curiosity and something darker drove him even closer to her. "A hacker and an MMA fighter?" he asked softly.

She stared at him, and he wanted to delve deeper into her green-eyed gaze.

She nodded her head slightly and stepped back again. "Yes," she said, her face turning away. "Not that it's any of your…business."

The pause had come because she'd seen his leg scar, and like so many others, tried to do the oh-so-fucking polite thing by ignoring it.

His lips compressed. Message received. The lady wasn't interested. She probably only dated pretty boys. And he certainly wasn't pretty. Not anymore.

"Sorry," he said, giving her space. "I didn't mean to interrupt your workout." He turned away to look for the gym manager to get set up.

"Jake," she said, a heavy sigh in her voice.

He looked over his shoulder, and then steeled himself against the soft look in her eyes. Was that worry creasing her brow?

"Look, I'm sorry," she said. She ran a hand over her braid. "I wasn't trying to be rude. I've just got a lot on my mind."

He turned to face her, unable to help himself, his instinct to protect kicking in. "Anything I can do?"

She opened her mouth as if to speak, but then her eyes shuttered and she shook her head. "I'm good."

He stepped back without comment, letting her pass as she strode to the women's changing room.

Off-limits, he reminded himself.

Dani shook off her unnerving reaction to Jake and hit the showers. She needed to stay away from him, no matter how well he filled out a t-shirt, or how much his heated eyes turned her insides to jelly.

The twisting scar on his leg looked painful and red. It must have happened recently. What had caused that type of injury? It didn't matter, she reminded herself. It wasn't like she was going to get to know him.

She figured being a Navy SEAL meant women threw themselves at Jake all the time. Well, no matter how many muscles he had, she wasn't throwing anything at him.

Except maybe a pair of sunglasses to hide those eyes of his. And a large hoodie to hide those shoulders. Or maybe just a giant snowsuit to cover all of him up.

She grimaced while she dried her hair. Lieutenant Jake Harrison was a distraction she could do without. The last time she'd been so distracted by a man it had left her bleeding and running for her life. She'd vowed to never let anyone else do that to her again. It's why she trained so hard to be able to defend herself.

After she finished dressing, she checked her phone again. No calls.

Tassia wasn't answering her phone, neither her office nor her cell. She could be in a meeting, but some instinct made Dani call her friend's cell once more. It went straight to voicemail.

"Tass, you're going to make me dinner for a week for not picking up your phone. Just call and let me know you're okay."

Once Dani made it into work with no word from Tass, she called the Public Prosecution's office and was told that Tassia hadn't come in yet. Her heart sank with the news. She went straight down the hall to Chuck's office and rapped on his door.

"What's up, Dani?" he asked. He cradled a mug of coffee in his hands.

"Tassia's missing." She hadn't meant to blurt it out like that.

He set the mug down. "Tell me everything."

After she had, he sat in the chair with his brows raised. "Let me get this straight. She's twenty-seven years old. She had a hot date last night and she hasn't made it into work yet. Have I got everything?"

Her face heated. "I know it's not much, but my gut tells me something's not right."

"Okay, Tassia is pretty reliable and it's not like her to miss work. What's this guy's name?"

"Vadim Levkov. I've tried searching for him, but…" She stopped when she saw him scrub a hand over his face. "It's not just because he's Russian that I'm worried, Chuck."

"Remember when you were worried about Tassia because she dated that academic from—"

"He was Russian. He could have been connected to *them*."

Chuck took a deep breath and studied her for a moment. "I'll see what I can do, but tell me something. When was the last time you went on a date, Dani?"

She blinked. "What does that have to do with anything?"

"How long?" he asked gently. "A year? Two?"

She scowled. "I don't see the point in dating when I can't tell anyone who I really am."

He shook his head. "You can. There are people out there you can trust besides me."

"And what happens if Vladimir finds me?"

Chuck's face hardened. "We'll deal with him. We got you away from him before. And the people you work with now? They can help you, if you'd trust them."

What he was asking was too much. She raised her hands as if to block his words. "This isn't about me. It's about Tassia."

"That's just it, kid," Chuck said. "This *is* about you. You don't even know what a fun time is. I'm not sure you've ever known. Your friend is out living the normal life of a young woman. You should try it sometime."

She slumped back into her seat. "You think I should

have a one-night stand?"

It was Chuck's turn to hold up his hands. "This conversation is fast moving into territory that I do not want to set foot in." He leaned back in his chair. "But, Dani…you do need to get a life."

Dani spent the rest of the morning fuming over Chuck's words, even as her worry increased when she still couldn't reach her friend. She realized that while she may need a life, she also knew when to listen to her gut. It had saved her too often to ignore it. And right now, her gut screamed at her to find Tassia.

She was picking up her cellphone again when her desk phone rang.

Mike was on the line. "Sorry I couldn't be there today. Did you get the stuff I left for you?"

She nodded even though he couldn't see it. "I finished the protocols you asked me to do and I'm up to speed on all the admin duties." Boring, easy, and boring. She hoped all the jobs weren't like this.

"Fast work. Good. Then I've got your first assignment," Mike said. "We've got a couple of newbies I need you to set up on the network."

"Can do," Dani said. "I've got admin access."

"They're the new field operators. They're waiting for you up on six." He hung up without saying goodbye.

Dani grabbed the case containing the gear she'd need

and went up to the sixth floor where the operators worked. She hadn't had a chance to try out her new passkey yet, and should have been excited to see into the vaulted interior workings of the sixth floor, but her mind was focused on how she could track down Tassia. Better yet, maybe she should try tracking down the mysterious Vadim.

Her thoughts left her friend as she entered the field operators' domain. An admin desk guarded the lair. A red-haired woman with gray at the temples manned it, her hatchet nose raised as she regarded Dani with suspicion.

"ID," she said.

Dani raised her badge and an eyebrow at the unsmiling woman. "I'm here to set up the two new operators on the network."

"Go on in," she said, and buzzed the interior door open.

Dani swung into the next room, where about ten desks, each housing a monitor and keyboard, lined the room. Maps decorated the wall opposite the full-length windows overlooking the busy street below. Oddly, the room was empty.

At the far end of the room was an open door. She walked forward and heard voices coming from beyond it. One voice in particular, actually. It was Mr. Knight's.

"...trafficking and suspected terrorist connections."

Trafficking and terrorism? What did that have to do with network security? She could see the end of a conference table, but no one was visible from her angle. She moved closer to the door, intending to knock and announce her presence, but she hesitated, her curiosity about E.D.G.E. leading her to listen a bit longer.

"What about local authorities?" That was Jake's voice.

"So far they're in the dark about this op." Papers shuffled. "We need eyes on target. Koven and Gordon, you set up surveillance. Harrison and Lafayette, you'll relieve them—"

"Sir?"

"Yes, Harrison?"

Jake appeared in the doorway. His head tilted and eyebrows rose as he looked at her. "Someone's at the door."

Merde, she'd been caught eavesdropping. Dani swallowed and stepped forward. Six field operators sat around the conference table while Mr. Knight stood at the head. All looked at her and she wanted to hide from Mr. Knight's direct gaze. But seriously, trafficking and terrorists? What was going on? Her questions about E.D.G.E. kept piling up.

Chuck sat at the table, disapproval heavy on his square face, and she wanted to shrink a little.

"Yes, Everett?" Knight asked her, interrupting her thoughts.

"Mike told me to set up the new people on the network."

"That would be us." Rhys popped up behind Jake. "We're the FNGs."

Dani frowned her question at Jake.

"Fucking new guys," Jake stage whispered back. The operators behind him all laughed and the tension broke.

"Right," Dani said.

"Everett?" Mr. Knight called before she could leave.

"Don't repeat anything you may or may not have heard in here."

"Yes, sir." She blew out a breath when Jake shut the door behind them, blocking out any further conversation. He gestured to a pair of desks against the wall, away from the windows. "We can use these."

She nodded as Jake walked to the desk. Both he and Rhys had dressed down today, wearing t-shirts and jeans. Jake's black tee stretched across his broad shoulders and his jeans molded to the contours of a very nice butt.

Rhys coughed and she saw the twinkle in his eye. Her cheeks heated. How unprofessional to be caught ogling someone.

She went to the unit at the first desk and entered the protocols E.D.G.E. demanded before any employee could have full access. She huffed a breath when she saw both Jake and Rhys rated full clearance even though they'd just started.

She did Rhys first, setting up passwords, fingerprints, and retinal scans. It didn't take long, but both men kept silent and it weighed on her. "I really didn't hear anything, beyond the setup of surveillance," she said.

"I believe you," Rhys said. His smile warmed Dani and her shoulders relaxed a little.

"I need your hand." She took it and placed his index finger on the imprint pad. She tapped in a code.

"Jake and I noticed you fighting this morning," Rhys said.

Jake stiffened where he stood leaning against the wall. Dani drew her eyes back to her screen. Had they been talking about her?

She nodded, but didn't say anything. She hadn't known Rhys was there, but then, she hadn't seen much beyond Jake and his biceps when she'd gotten out of the ring.

"Where'd you learn to fight?" Rhys asked as she manipulated his hand to get his thumbprint next.

"I used to work at an MMA gym," she said.

He smiled and nodded. "You looked like you could handle yourself. Ever been in a real fight?"

Dani busied herself with her laptop. She'd been in more fights than she could count and had the knife scars to prove it. That was the gang way of life. And Vladimir hadn't minded her learning to fight, as long as she never fought *him*. Now she continued to train hard so she could fight anyone and survive.

"No," she said finally.

Time to shut this conversation down. She dragged out the retinal scanner and positioned it on the desk, but she didn't miss the eye contact between Rhys and Jake, or Jake's frown.

"Place your chin here," she said, pointing at the small strap. "Focus on the red light and don't blink."

Within seconds it was done.

"Thank you, ma'am," Rhys said. "I've got to get to work now." He went back to the conference room and left her alone with Jake.

She turned to Jake, keeping what she hoped was a professional smile on her face. "Your turn."

His narrowed gaze studied her and her smile faltered. He took Rhys's place at the desk and still didn't say anything.

Fine. She could do cold and calculated with the best of them. He might be a high-and-mighty Navy SEAL, but she was battle-hardened in her own way. Maybe she didn't have formal training, but his tough-guy glare wasn't going to scare her.

Okay, maybe it freaked her out a little, but she'd be damned if she let it show.

She kept her face and tone professional as she asked him to type in a password and his information.

"Hand," she said, holding hers out. As he placed his large calloused one in hers, a little zing of heat ripped from her palm to her chest. She swallowed and placed his index finger on the imprint pad.

"Where'd you get the knife scars?" Jake asked.

She jerked. The imprint didn't take and she tapped a code into the machine to reset it. She used the time to steady her voice. "What do you mean?" She repositioned his finger and steeled herself against his next question.

"You lied to Rhys when you said you'd never fought." He paused. "I need to be able to trust everyone on this team."

She didn't look at him as she set up to take his thumbprint. "I'm just an IT tech. It doesn't matter if you trust me or not."

"You want to be a field operator."

She shot him a sharp glance. "How do you know that?"

"I looked up your file." He wasn't the slightest bit apologetic. "And it left me with a lot of questions. They want me to be a team leader here. If I take the job, then I want to be able to trust every member of my team…even the IT tech."

His eyes softened and suddenly Dani couldn't speak, couldn't avoid his compassionate gaze. His next words twisted something inside her.

"You don't have to lie to me."

Dani stared at him, her teeth clenched tight. She couldn't tell him the truth. The more people who knew her history, the more chances that someone would slip up and she'd have to run again.

She put on her best professional smile. "Please put your chin in the strap and look at the red light."

His lips pressed tight before he blanked his face and set his chin in the strap.

After work that day, Dani went into Tassia's apartment. It looked the same as it had in the morning, except for the note on the kitchen table.

Danielle,

I've gone to Europe. I'll be in touch in a few weeks. Don't worry about me.

Tassia

What the *hell*? Dani dropped the note and raced to her friend's bedroom. Clothes spilled from her closet and drawers. A quick check revealed the suitcase under her bed was gone.

Dani slumped onto Tass's bed. This didn't make any sense. Tassia wouldn't just up and leave her job. Her desk appeared cleared, as if she'd taken everything with her, but the bedside table still held her Kindle.

The hair stood up on the back of Dani's neck. Tass would never leave on a vacation without her Kindle. She slowly swiveled her head, taking in the room again. Her friend's jewelry box rested on her dresser.

Dani opened it. Tassia's favorite charm bracelet, the silver one her parents had given her for graduation, sat on top.

Something was very wrong.

She called the Public Prosecution's office only to be told that Tassia had called in and requested emergency leave.

Dani clenched her fists. There was no way her friend would leave for Europe without talking to her first. She went back to the note in the kitchen. It was in Tass's handwriting, but upon closer examination the writing had a bit of a wobble to it, as if the hand that wrote it was trembling. And Tass never called her Danielle. Never.

Dani picked up the phone and called the police.

CHAPTER 4

D ani had avoided the gym that morning and opted for a long run and getting in early to work instead. She needed to figure out her next step. She'd spent last evening at the police station filling out a missing persons report on Tassia.

Unfortunately, with a note in Tassia's handwriting and phone calls to her place of work saying she was going on leave, the police didn't have a whole lot of options. The overworked detective had told her to contact him if she remembered anything else or heard from Tassia again.

She'd known the police were a longshot, but she had to try things the legal way first. She owed that to Chuck. Now, though, it would be up to Dani to track Tassia down, and she needed to start with the mysterious Vadim Levkov.

The elevator dinged as the doors opened on her floor at E.D.G.E. Dani made a beeline to her desk and set to work. But no matter what she tried, she couldn't find a Vadim Levkov that matched what she knew about him. She only found the four men she'd noted previously, and none of them made sense. One was a teenager on Twitter who lived in Ottawa and two were sixty plus. One was in his forties, but as attractive as a dancing bear.

A sudden thought stole her breath. She slowly typed Vladimir Levkov into her program. Within minutes she had a lead. A Vladimir Levkov worked for the Volga Group, a company that imported and exported high-end art according to its simple two-page website. She could glean nothing else useful from the site.

She tried not to worry. Vladimir was a common name. So common that it was also the name of the man with a starring role in her nightmares. She shook off her fear and dove back into the research.

If this was the right guy, then perhaps the Volga Group was the company the Public Prosecution was building a case against, the one Tass had mentioned. It would explain why Tassia didn't want to talk about the mysterious Vadim.

And perhaps that's why he'd given her a different name. Because if he worked at the company she was helping to investigate, and anyone found out they were dating, it would ruin the investigation. Tass would be demoted or fired.

Dani chewed on her lip. Her instincts told her Tassia

was in trouble. She didn't know how to prove it, but her stomach churned at the thought of giving up.

She glanced around. No one was in yet, and she needed more information. She drummed her fingers on her desk, debating the pros and cons of delving past Volga's firewall while at E.D.G.E.

Screw it.

The consequences didn't matter if Tass was in trouble. Her friend needed her.

Dani dug into the company's site and found the firewalls protecting their server. She sat up straight, her fingers stilling over the keyboard. These were high-grade firewalls. Much stronger than a typical commercial company should have. These were something she'd only seen when hacking government or banking sites.

"Everett." The rough but familiar voice came from the doorway to the field operators' lair.

She jumped and swiveled to face Jake. He stood by the heavy steel door, the stairway behind him filled with shadows. Her heart thumped hard in her chest and she wasn't sure if it was because he'd almost caught her or because Jake's piercing gray eyes seemed to uncover all of her secrets.

She wet her dry lips. "Did you need something?"

Something flickered in his gaze and her breath caught in her throat at the predatory gleam. Then his eyes cleared and he nodded at her laptop. "I'm being denied access to our server. Have you hooked me in yet?"

She mentally groaned, but pasted a professional smile on her face. In truth, she'd forgotten to give him access after their encounter yesterday. She hated how he affected her, making her brain short circuit. "I'll have it sorted in a few minutes."

"Thanks." He stood studying her for a moment, almost as if he knew she'd been contemplating something illegal. She finally arched a brow at him, silently asking him if he was done. His lips compressed before he left the room. The heavy door swooshed shut and locked with a click.

Her lips twisted. It was too dangerous to hack into Volga Group from an E.D.G.E. computer. She'd have to get her information the old-fashioned way. She needed to access the Volga server from inside its own firewalls, which meant she needed to break into their offices tonight.

Dani was up to something. It wasn't just the way she'd jumped when Jake had called her name, but the way her eyes kept sliding from him to her screen, almost as if she were afraid he would see what was there.

Should he go back and confront her? He shook his head and took the steps two at a time up the spiral staircase leading to a workroom on the field operators' floor. His leg only protested a little, which he ignored. He pushed through the steel door and went to the desk he'd claimed.

Beyond this room lay the lounge, and beyond that a small room with a couple of cots. He'd explored this floor yesterday and had been surprised to see a well-stocked weapons room, besides the conference room and the workroom where Dani had connected him to the network.

Or she was supposed to have connected him to the network. Apparently, she'd forgotten. He must have gotten under her skin. He smiled. Good. Because she sure as hell was under his. He'd had to take a cold shower before bed last night. The image of Dani in her shorts and sports bra had made his skin heat. All that silky skin, those smooth muscles exposed. He wanted to unbraid her dark hair and feel it trail over his chest as she rode him.

He clenched his fists and broke the spell. He needed a long run. Or maybe another cold shower. Because he refused to get involved with this woman, even just a fling. She had warning labels written all over her.

And really, flings were all he did anyway. The life of a spec ops soldier didn't allow for much else. He didn't have time to worry about a woman. Of course, he knew guys who were married, but he figured either they'd found a one-in-a-million woman or the divorce was coming soon.

Either way, it was time to put Dani out of his head and focus on the upcoming op. He tapped a few keys on the computer and his password worked this time. He pulled up the details on the surveillance he and Rhys would conduct today.

He memorized the faces of the targets, as well as maps of the city. He calculated possible escape routes for him and Rhys to drive if anything went down. The company they would watch today was rumored to be part of the Bratva, the Russian mafia, a cover for human and drug trafficking.

From the reports, they were brutal and vicious but smart, at least until recently. Apparently, Quebec's Public Prosecution was looking into them, but was having trouble keeping witnesses.

The Canadian government had asked for help with the case. It was actually a small job, an easy training mission according to Knight, but he figured it would be a good one for Jake and Rhys to get to know the other members of E.D.G.E.

An easy training mission. Jake snorted and quickly changed his line of thinking before he jinxed them. He'd never before considered the Russians an "easy training mission," and he wouldn't start now.

A couple of hours later, he came across a term that his imperfect knowledge of Russian didn't cover, and decided to seek Dani out. He should just Google it, but her personnel file had indicated a fluency in Russian. He wanted to find out why she knew that language so well. He guessed she probably wouldn't answer, but he could watch the play of emotions cross her face and see if he could solve more of the puzzle of her.

He probably wouldn't like the answers he found, but he couldn't stop probing at her armored exterior. He went back downstairs to find her, but another IT tech said she'd gone home sick.

He went back upstairs to his desk, ignoring the twinge

in his leg and the disappointment in his gut.

Dani sat on a bench across the street from a brownstone building on Boulevard Rene-Levesque. According to its website, the Volga Group took up the fourth floor of the eight-story building. The company had warehouses down by the docks as well, but Dani figured any information that might interest her would be found on the computers in the main office.

She sat with her tablet and a latte, her sunglasses hiding the fact that she watched the front doors. There were two side doors, both leading to the back alley filled with dumpsters, not somewhere anyone would go for lunch.

She crossed her legs, her only pair of black heels gleaming in the noon sunshine. She'd told Mike she wasn't feeling well and had gone home early. Then she'd gone to Tassia's place and raided her closet. A trim black jacket and matching skirt hugged her figure and restricted her movements. She looked like every other businesswoman on the street, brainy and defenseless.

People started to stream from the front doors of the building. She pretended to consult her tablet as she sipped her latte and scanned the lunch crowd. She hadn't recognized anyone so far. It was almost twelve-thirty. Most people would have left for lunch by now.

She was about to stand when she froze like a deer scenting danger.

Two men stomped through the glass doors. They were boulders on legs. People gave them plenty of space as they strode down the street. The way they moved with utter confidence and an inherent cruelty made the hair stand up on the back of her neck.

Boris Gromov and his brother Ivan didn't look like stereotypical businessmen. They looked exactly like what they were: the Rusakov family enforcers.

It had been years since she'd last seen them. They stuck near Dmitri and Vladimir, doing whatever was asked of them, like well-trained jackels. She remembered the strength of their bruising grip on her arms, holding her while Vladimir ranted about her speaking too long with a fellow computer geek. He'd only slapped her that time. The brothers had held her still the whole time.

No, no, no, she chanted to herself. This couldn't be happening. She swallowed against a suddenly dry throat.

Please, don't let the Rusakovs be doing business with the Volga Group.

Though now Dani was pretty sure the Volga Group was the company the Public Prosecution office, and therefore Tassia, was investigating.

She shook herself mentally. Now was not the time to get freaked. Tassia needed her. Dani just had to follow her plan.

After the Gromov brothers were out of sight, she stood up and smoothed her skirt before clicking her way across the street and into the building. She had to walk slower than normal, thanks to the stilettos Tassia had convinced her she needed. Her ankles only wobbled once.

Inside the elevator, she pressed the buttons for the third and fourth floors. When the doors opened on the third floor, she popped her head out to scan the area, seeing a hallway with office doors at either end and a communal washroom across from the elevators. No security cameras in the hall, just the one in the elevator. Then, she rode the elevator to four.

The doors opened to reveal a large sign announcing the Volga Group, and another for the real estate company that shared the floor with them. More communal washrooms stood between the two companies. Volga Group was to the left and had glass doors with a keycard panel. The doors stood open at the moment.

Her heart thumped hard inside her chest and she discreetly wiped her palms on her skirt.

For Tassia.

Modern black leather-and-steel furniture and abstract art featuring slashes of red decorated the lobby. Was this the kind of art they imported? Most of it looked like an angry child had thrown paint on a canvas.

She minced her way to the receptionist sitting behind an imposing black lacquered desk. The woman wore a duplicate of Tassia's little black suit, though she seemed much more comfortable in it than Dani did.

The receptionist was of Asian descent, and had her black hair swept into an elegant twist at the back of her head. Something Dani would never be able to do on her own. She looked to be about Dani's age and had a distinctive mole on her jawline.

"May I help you?" she asked.

"*Oui*," Dani said, speaking in French. "I'm here to see Mr. Taylor." Dani checked her watch.

"I'm sorry," the receptionist said and tilted her head. "We don't have anyone by that name who works here."

Dani widened her eyes and took a step back. "You don't?" She looked around as if only now taking in the room. As she did so, she noted the lack of security cameras inside the reception area. Excellent.

"*Zut alors!*" Dani said, expressing surprise. "I believe I'm in the wrong office. I'm supposed to be next door. *Pardonnez-moi.*"

She left and pretended to go into the real estate offices before taking the stairs down to the lobby. No cameras in the stairwell and the doors weren't locked. Hopefully they'd stay that way after closing.

She strode out into the sunshine, her shoulders loosening with each step away from the building. She walked to the nearest cafe with a view of the building to grab another latte. Step one of her plan was complete. She figured she had a few hours to wait before implementing step two. Patience was a necessary virtue for a thief.

CHAPTER 5

Patience was a necessary virtue for a sniper, and also apparently for an E.D.G.E. operator staking out a building. At least Jake wasn't freezing his nuts off in the mountains of the Hindu Kush, waiting motionless for the enemy to appear.

This afternoon, he and Rhys sat in the back of a white bakery van parked near a cafe, watching and listening to the Volga Group across the street. A bank of computers and high-tech equipment decorated one side of the van. Mike, the IT guru, had explained how everything worked and then left them to it. Both of them had used enough tech that they were completely comfortable with the surveillance toys.

Jake stretched his legs and sighed. Even though he was

warm, could move, and had his buddy to talk to, he'd still rather be in the Hindu Kush with his team, doing something worthwhile. Something his country needed. Watching a company to see if anything illegal was going on just didn't compare, no matter how comfortable he was.

"Leg bothering you?" Rhys asked. He sat in the other chair watching his own set of monitors.

"Nah," Jake said. He'd never admit how much it ached, but Rhys knew that. "I'm bored and wondering what we're really doing here."

"We're trying out the life of a spy. And I, for one, like this luxury." Rhys slurped his coffee and rested his feet on the table holding the monitors. "You have to admit, it's nothing to sneer at."

Jake narrowed his eyes. "You're not serious. Do you really think we should stay with these overblown PIs?"

"They're more than that," Rhys said. "They saved our asses last year, remember? They can't be all bad. Besides, we can't be on the teams forever."

"No, but we can work *with* the teams."

Rhys snorted. "You like working behind a desk?"

Jake stiffened and focused on the monitors, looking for his targets. "That isn't the point."

"We could do good work here too," Rhys said.

"You mean *me*," Jake replied without looking at his friend. His leg ramped up the pain as if in protest and he gritted his teeth. "We're going back. The team is almost finished training for the next deployment and you're going with them. And I…I'll do whatever needs to be done."

Rhys sipped his coffee. "Just don't—"

Something on the monitor caught Jake's eye. "What the hell?"

Rhys's feet hit the deck. "What's up?"

Jake watched the monitor closely, following the sleek brunette coming toward them. His lips twitched when she wobbled on her spiky heels. Not practical, but they showcased some amazing legs. She carried a large tote bag. Why did women have such giant purses?

"Earth to College?" Rhys interrupted his wayward thoughts.

Jake snapped his mind into gear. There definitely weren't distractions like this in the Hindu Kush. He pointed to the screen. "Isn't that the new IT tech? What's her name?" He paused as if he hadn't memorized everything he could find in her very small file. "Danielle. Danielle Everett."

Rhys glanced sideways at him and raised an eyebrow.

"What?" Jake asked.

Rhys didn't bother to answer, and they watched her enter the cafe near the van's location.

"Why would she change her clothes and come across town for coffee?" Jake asked.

Rhys sent him another sideways look. "She changed clothes?"

"She was wearing a man's suit this morning." Jake blanked his face while Rhys continued to watch him knowingly. "We're trained to notice details, remember? Anyway, she had to do a task for me this morning."

Rhys leaned back in his chair, his lips twitching. "A task?"

"What? Are you a freaking parrot today?" Jake watched Dani stroll into the coffee shop and ignored Rhys's smirk. Once Dani was out of sight, he let out a deep breath and focused. "Something's off," he said.

Rhys dropped his smirk. "She got caught hacking E.D.G.E. files two days ago, and now she's coming out of the same building we're staking out?" He shook his head. "That doesn't look good. We should call it in."

Jake agreed, but paused a moment. "She'll most likely be fired if we do." He wasn't sure why that bothered him, but the image of her in the gym yesterday morning popped into his mind. She'd been worried about something, and that had been before she'd gotten into the office. "Wait out on this one, Lucky. I want to see how it plays."

Rhys studied his face for a moment. "Roger that."

Jake rubbed his leg. "I suddenly feel like a coffee."

Rhys grinned. "Good hunting."

As Jake entered the cafe, he stepped to the side and scanned the occupants, knowing better than to pause in a doorway silhouetted against the light. It was a diner-style cafe with creamy walls and a hardwood floor, hosting a long bar with stools, booths against the far wall and a few tables near the front.

Seven people sat in the room. Four in the booths, two separately at the bar, and one lady in a tight black suit with great legs sitting at a table by the front window.

Dani held a book in front of her face, a romance novel with some bare-chested guy in a kilt on the cover. He almost snorted. He continued to the bar as if he hadn't seen her, and ordered a coffee from the waitress.

"To stay?" she asked, her French accent thick.

Jake thought about it. From the corner of his eye he could see Dani's stiff posture. She looked like a scared rabbit. She'd probably have a heart attack if he stayed. It would be smarter to leave and then see what she did after knowing he was in the area. Would she scurry away? He found that he wanted her to be here for a legitimate reason. He wanted to go and ask her.

"To go," he said gruffly. He tried never to let emotions play into his decisions. He'd learned that even before the Navy.

He grabbed the coffee and meant to walk out the door, but instead found himself standing in front of her table.

"Dani," he said, wondering what the hell he was doing.

Her shoulders slumped and he wanted to laugh. Then she straightened and lowered the book. "Hey, Jake. What are you doing here?"

"My hotel is around the corner," he lied. "Just stopping in for a coffee before heading off to that assignment you're not supposed to know about."

She blushed and he liked the spark of fire in her eyes. "What about you?" he asked.

"I'm here for the amazing *poutine*," she said. As if on cue, a waitress brought over a plate of thick-cut french fries with gravy and…

"Is that cheese?" he asked, sidetracked by the delicious smell of the gravy.

"It's *poutine*," she said, pronouncing it *puht-in*. "Fries, light gravy, and cheese curds." She pushed the plate toward him. "Try it."

He sat down in the chair opposite her and picked up a crisp fry dripping with gravy and ensnared in melted cheese. "Cheese curds?"

"*Poutine*'s a Canadian staple. Right up there with maple syrup, bacon, and beer. You have to try it."

He grinned at her enthusiasm for what looked like a heart attack on a plate, and ate the fry. The savory flavor exploded in his mouth and his stomach rumbled for more. He snagged another fry. Dani smiled at him. "I told you," she said, pulling her plate back.

"You went home sick," Jake said. He almost cursed himself when the light went out of her eyes and her smile disappeared. He hadn't meant to blurt it out like that, but he had to know why she'd lied about going home.

Her eyes flicked away and then back, assessing him. "My friend is missing," she said, a hint of desperation in her voice.

He went on alert. "Have you told the police?"

She nodded. "There's not enough evidence for them to do anything right now."

"So *you're* going to do something." His lips firmed. "Something illegal?"

Her chin jutted out. "I'm just waiting to meet someone who might be able to help. There's nothing illegal about that."

Instinct told him she was holding back information—a lot of information. He looked around the diner. This was not the place to question her.

"I've only been at E.D.G.E. a couple of days," he said, "but it seems to me you should ask your friends there to help you." She didn't say anything. So he tried again. "I could help you, Dani."

She froze, as if unsure what to do with his offer.

He sighed and stood up, snagging one last fry and giving her a salute with it. "I hope you find your friend."

Her face softened. "Thank you," she said.

He left the cafe, coffee in hand. He made sure she didn't see him get back into the van. Now, it was time to see if the rabbit ran.

Hours later, Dani finally left the coffee shop. Jake watched her while Rhys watched the front doors of the building.

"She's heading into the building," Jake said quietly.

Rhys nodded. "Have her in sight."

They watched as she hurried toward the revolving doors. Her ankle wobbled and she toppled, crashing into an Asian woman whose purse flew in the fall. Dani's arms waved around as she helped the smaller woman to her feet and helped gather the woman's purse and belongings. Then they parted ways and Dani strode through the revolving doors.

Jake frowned, tension thrumming through him. "What just happened there?"

Dani closed her book with a sniff. She loved happy endings. Too bad life couldn't be like a romance novel. But there was no hero waiting in the wings to rescue her. She'd learned that a long time ago. She'd had to rescue herself.

The darkness of the third-floor ladies washroom was only broken by her penlight. She put it in her mouth while she shoved her book into her large tote. She'd been sitting in this toilet stall since five. She checked her watch. Just past eleven at night.

Her muscles protested when she stood up and opened the door. She spent a few minutes stretching before shucking her jacket and skirt. Underneath, she wore black leggings rolled up past her thighs, which she proceeded to pull down to cover her legs. On top she had a black, long-sleeved stretch tee. She swapped out her heels for a pair of black-on-black sneakers. A black ski mask completed her breaking-and-entering ensemble.

This floor had no security cameras, so no one could track her. She zipped her tote and left the bathroom, heart pounding.

Five years ago, she'd sworn to never break the law again. To never again travel that slippery slope that had led her straight to Vladimir. But that had been before Tassia had gone missing. And besides, it wasn't as if she was stealing anything. Dani didn't really consider hacking against the law, unless you did something illegal with the information. And tonight she only wanted a peek at Volga's information. The breaking-and-entering part was a necessary evil, so she could be inside the company's firewall.

She'd thought for sure she'd have to abandon her plan when Jake had entered the cafe. But he'd left without harassing her about what she was doing. His smile when he'd tried her *poutine* had softened his harsh edges and relaxed him. She wanted to see him smile again. Her cheeks heated. He wouldn't smile if he could see her now. Mr. Straight-and-Narrow would definitely not approve of what she was doing.

Had he been right? Should she ask someone at E.D.G.E. to help her?

No, she couldn't. She didn't have any real friends there except for Chuck, and he didn't think there was an issue. And even if he did, he'd want to do things by the book, which her gut said would take too long for Tass. Dani had only herself, no matter what Jake said.

Her doubts added to her tension, tightening muscles and occupying her thoughts. She needed complete focus and she couldn't let Jake, his smile, or his biceps take up any more of her time.

She went to the stairs and crept up them, her penlight flashing over the concrete walls. The silence made her breathing seem louder and harsher than it was. At the fourth floor, she listened carefully before cracking the door open.

Silence and darkness. She pulled out the keycard she'd swiped from the receptionist earlier when she'd purposely knocked her purse over in front of the building. She was a little rusty at picking pockets, but the woman hadn't suspected anything.

She passed it over the card reader beside the office entrance. The click of the door unlatching sounded like a gunshot in the quiet. She slipped inside and trotted down the dark hall, keeping her penlight pointed at the floor as she read the names off the small plaques beside each office door.

Boris Gromov, VP of Marketing. And beside that one was Ivan Gromov's office. Apparently he was VP of Sales. They must have laughed at those titles. What was going on? She shivered and kept moving.

The next nameplate stated Vladimir Levkov, VP of Business Development. She panted as if running up a hill and focused on controlling her breathing.

If the Public Prosecutor was investigating the company for something, then Levkov's involvement with Tassia looked seriously suspicious. Even though Tassia couldn't have known that Vadim was really Vladimir, and connected to the company she investigated.

But then, if Levkov was who Dani thought he was, Tassia would have had a hard time resisting his charms. Dani prayed she was wrong.

Inside Levkov's office, Dani made sure to shut the blinds so her penlight wouldn't be seen from outside. She didn't turn on the lights—she didn't need to. The light from his computer monitor revealed his office as she touched his mouse to wake it. It asked for a password.

She pulled her laptop out of her tote, and after setting it beside his computer, she plugged it into his system. She'd recently upgraded the graphics processing card that would let her brute-force cracking code run faster on the GPU rather than the laptop's CPU. She set her program parameters and let it fly.

While her system went to work, she explored the office. A bookshelf held a few books on art, though dust covered them, as well as the rest of the empty shelf space. A check of his desk drawers revealed two pens, a pad of paper, and some receipts from a nearby Chinese restaurant. No pictures or anything personal sat anywhere in the office.

Dani frowned as her laptop beeped at her. It had taken all of two minutes to crack his password.

Kotyonok.

The Russian word for kitten. It was the pet name Vladimir had called her.

Ice traveled from her core outward, while her heart thundered in her ears. She closed her eyes and breathed deeply, trying to slow her racing heart. She should have followed Tass on her date rather than indulging her curiosity and cracking E.D.G.E.'s inner firewalls.

She ignored the impulse to run and forced herself to

go through Levkov's system. Though she knew that wasn't his real name. A few minutes later she sat back, frowning. Nothing. As far as she could tell, only video games had been played on this computer. Even the email was nonexistent.

What was going on here? She packed up her system and decided to dig deeper, her curiosity driving her as much as her need to find her friend. She walked down the hallway until she came to the corner office. The president of the company.

Dmitri Levkov.

She paled. She could no longer deny it. It wasn't the right last name, but the name Dmitri confirmed her suspicions. The Levkov name had to be a cover for Dmitri and Vladimir, the ruler and heir-apparent of the Rusakov family—one of the largest Russian mafia families in North America. She'd been hiding from the *Bratva* for five years now. The only reason she'd thought she was safe in Montreal was that Vladimir had been sent to Russia by his family as punishment.

For killing her.

He was obviously back and working in the family business again. And here she was, breaking into one of their offices. Nausea threatened to bring her to her knees.

"Just get the information, Dani," she muttered to herself.

Inside, she ran her fingers over the books decorating one wall. A small filing cabinet only held a few files of art transactions. She sat down at the large, polished wood desk and sighed.

Dmitri had a Cyrillic alphabet keyboard, which would make things more difficult, but not impossible. Her Russian reading skills were rusty, so she added a translating program from Russian to English before she started the cracking program.

As her system went to work, she checked Dmitri's desk. Nothing interesting, and she prayed for Tassia's sake that there was something more useful on his system than video games.

Her laptop came up with Dmitri's password and she set to work. She dug through his files, moving slowly because she had to translate what she was seeing. She tapped her fingers on the desk and glanced at the wall clock. 11:45. She bit her lip. She'd already been here longer than she wanted.

His email revealed sparse conversations with a couple of galleries in the city. Not enough for a healthy art-import business. There were a few messages from the Office of Public Prosecution relating their intent to investigate Volka.

The clock now said 12:15.

The back of her neck prickled with unease. Cutting off the email, she inserted a backdoor program into Dmitri's system so she could enter remotely, bypassing the major firewalls she'd found earlier. She bit her lip and surveyed the sparse office. Why have such sturdy firewalls if there wasn't anything to find? He must have information somewhere. Probably on a home computer or laptop. She needed to dig deeper.

She found files on imports and exports for the company

and a list of shipping records. She downloaded that onto a flash drive as well as her laptop. Sweat trickled down her back. She needed to get out of here, but she wanted to explore just a bit more.

She did a quick scan of his calendar and sucked in a breath. Dmitri Levkov, business leader, was hosting a party this weekend. The details included a guest list of over a hundred people.

She bit her lip and then added a name to the list.

D. Everett.

CHAPTER 6

J ake kept his Sig Sauer P226 in the holster at the small of his back as he ran silently down the stairs to the fourth floor. He didn't expect any action, and he could handle any security he might encounter with his hands. He'd much prefer a guard to wake up with a headache than to kill an innocent man just doing his job.

Before he opened the door to the fourth floor, he keyed his mic.

"Zero, this is Alpha, over," he said quietly.

Rhys's voice came over the earpiece. "Alpha this is Zero. Five by five, over."

"Zero, I'm heading in. Wait out." He entered the dark hall and made his way down to the Volga Group, one of the business fronts of the Rusakov family. He pulled out a metal piece of tech about the size of a credit card that Mike had given him. He swiped it over the keycard scanner and the doors clicked open.

After a cursory look around, he planted bugs under the receptionist desk and in the phone. Apparently with these cool toys, Mike and his team would be able to remotely access Volga's servers. They'd wanted it in an innocuous system, figuring they might be detected in the VP's offices.

"Zero, the rats are deployed. Over."

"Copy that, Alpha. Exfil. Over."

"Roger, Zero. Wilco. Out." Jake went back to the stairwell, planning on heading back to the roof, where he would rappel down to the street. But as he touched the door, a flicker of light from Volga's hallway made him pause. Someone with a flashlight was coming this way.

He faded into the shadows near the bathrooms and waited, wondering who else was breaking and entering tonight, and why.

"Zero," he breathed. "We have trouble. Over."

"Define trouble. Over." Rhys's voice sounded resigned. Did he think Jake went looking for it?

"Looks like another nighttime visitor, Zero. Will investigate. Wait out."

A figure in black wearing a ski mask like his paused on the other side of the glass doors, in the shadows, waiting like a mouse to see if a cat was around.

The figure was slight. Female. She knew not to rush and hadn't set off any alarms. She'd obviously done this before.

She moved slightly and recognition flared through Jake. His lips compressed.

Danielle.

What was she up to?

Jake kept his muscles relaxed and his breathing unhurried. He could out-wait her. He wanted to see what she would do next.

Five minutes later, Jake smiled. Dani crept toward the glass doors and opened them quietly before cautiously stepping into the hall. She carried the large tote that she'd had earlier. Jake waited until the doors swung shut before showing himself.

"Nice night for a little breaking and entering," he said.

Dani's eyes rounded behind the mask. She dropped her bag and swung her leg into a roundhouse kick. He blocked it, and the following punch-kick combination. She was good, but not good enough.

He grabbed her arm and twisted it up behind her. "What are you doing here?"

She stiffened, but didn't answer him. Suddenly, she went limp and became dead weight in his arms. Jake eased her to the floor, a plan forming in his mind.

He let go of her arm. "Did you really just faint?" he asked skeptically.

She swung a punch at his dick. He jerked aside while she leapt to her feet and spun into a back kick thrust to his stomach. He let it hit with a grunt and didn't grab her leg to subdue her, though he easily could have. She had to think she'd bested him.

Dani grabbed her tote and sprinted for the stairwell.

Now, it was time to see where the rabbit ran.

Dani nibbled on her pencil as she stared at the files she'd dug up on Dmitri's computer.

She yawned and sipped at her glass of wine. It was closing in on two o'clock in the morning, and she should get some sleep or she'd be a mess at work tomorrow. She'd just been too wired when she first got home. Jumping at every sound, thinking Jake had followed her. Eventually she'd changed into a tank top and boxers and poured herself a glass of wine. Jake couldn't know it was her.

Could he?

She shook her head. When he'd first stepped out of the shadows, her heart had leapt so hard she hadn't been able to recognize his voice. But she'd known who it was after he'd spoken the second time, when he'd shoved her arm up her back. She rolled her shoulder where it still twinged. He'd been fast and strong. She'd never fought someone like him. She shivered at the thought of all that strength.

She gulped her wine. Enough of that. If he'd suspected who she was, then he'd have already shown up here. No. She'd gotten away with it.

Barely.

Now she just had to figure out what Dmitri and Vladimir were hiding and how it connected to Tassia.

She stared at the Excel database of import and export

transactions. The import side had about twenty items come in every six to eight weeks, but there was no reference to what they were or how much each cost.

Each piece of art should be a different price, but it looked like the same amount of money was paid no matter the amount of items shipped and received.

The export side of things was even stranger. The company took advantage of the same shipping crate and sent back only one or two items each time. These few items usually paid almost as much as the entire batch of imported ones.

Dani leaned back in her desk chair. Dmitri wasn't an art dealer. The Rusakov family mainly trafficked drugs. There was no way they'd gone legit. She ran her fingers through her hair.

Her skin prickled as a cool draft brushed over her bare shoulders. She whirled in her desk chair. Jake stood by the balcony door in black combat gear and boots. A belt with various pouches on it emphasized his narrow waist. He no longer wore the ski mask.

She screamed and chucked her empty wine glass at him. He dodged it and stepped closer. Her heart thudded hard in her chest. She threw her wireless mouse, a romance novel, and her mug of pencils, her hand scrabbling along her desk for something else.

"Would you relax?" he said in between dodging projectiles. "I'm not going to hurt you."

She picked up her cellphone, changed her mind, and put it back down. "Like I'm supposed to believe you?" She grabbed a glass paperweight and heaved it. "You broke into my apartment!"

He caught the paperweight easily and set it on a side table. "Like you broke into the Volga Group tonight?"

Dani stilled, her mind racing. "What do you want?"

He studied her for a minute, and she remembered she stood there in her skimpy black tank and boxers. She crossed her arms. "I *said*, what do you want?"

He sighed. "I'm not sure, really. I should have reported you immediately, but..." He rubbed a hand through his dark hair, his gray eyes on hers. "I'm giving you a chance. I want the truth. Why did you break in? What were you doing?"

Dani stepped back. Could she trust him? Would he help her? She wasn't used to being able to depend on people; most had turned on her at some point.

But Chuck hadn't.

And neither had Tassia.

Tassia needed her, and everything Dani could do to help her, even if it included trusting Jake. Dani stared into his pale eyes so full of questions. He stood with his arms loose by his sides as he waited for her decision. It was as if she could feel him silently imploring her to trust him. She opened her mouth to explain when his gaze flicked to her laptop screen and the open files.

He scowled and his whole demeanor changed. Gone was the solid, compassionate man, and in his place stood a ruthless soldier.

"You hacked into their system?" He shook his head. "Do you know who these people are? What they're capable of?" He stepped in close, looming over her. She hadn't realized he was so tall, but this close she had to tilt her chin to keep eye contact.

She couldn't tell him that she knew the Rusakov family. That the prodigal son had been obsessed with her. He wouldn't understand. And he'd want to tell the others at E.D.G.E.

She'd been a fool to think she could trust him. He was a SEAL who got the job done, no matter the cost.

He stepped closer, as if trying to intimidate her. "Tell me, do you?" he ordered.

She refused to back up, just lifted her chin higher. "I don't know what you're talking about."

His lips twitched slightly before his face became cold again. "Seriously?" He now stood so close that if she took a deep breath her breasts would brush his chest. His voice lowered. "Do you realize what I could do to you?"

Her eyes widened, not at his words, but at his tone, and she sucked in a breath, putting their chests into contact for the briefest moment. Her nipples tightened and a different kind of tension curled through her. Jake glanced down and stilled.

He raised his head and heat darkened the gray of his eyes to molten steel. Dani wet her suddenly dry lips and his gaze tracked the movement. She no longer felt as if she were on trial, but rather as if she were being hunted by something dark and dangerous. Something sensual.

The air in the room thickened and she had to take deeper breaths, each one brushing her sensitive nipples against his shirt. Neither one of them moved away, their gazes locked on each other. She swallowed and curled her fingers to stop them from reaching for him.

She wanted to kiss him, needed for him to kiss her. It didn't matter that she didn't trust him. She wanted to feel him, the power of his hands on her.

No. She'd been too close to a powerful man before and it'd almost destroyed her. She spun away from him.

When she looked back, Jake stood on the far side of the room, all evidence of the seductive man gone and the ruthless soldier back in place. Her gaze traveled over him and paused on the front of his pants. She smirked. Well, maybe not *all* of the evidence had disappeared.

Her smile faded when she saw what he held. "What are you doing with my laptop?"

"See me first thing in the morning," he said gruffly, and left through her front door.

CHAPTER 7

J ake had skipped the gym that morning and now wished he hadn't. He'd wanted to avoid any possibility of seeing Dani, but his muscles protested not doing anything, especially after the restless night he'd had. He'd tossed and turned, thinking about Dani's skimpy tank top and the way her nipples had peaked when he'd been close.

He definitely had energy to burn. Maybe he'd drop the laptop off with Mike and go hit the bag in the operatives' gym on the fifth floor.

He found Mike in front of some serious tech gear, using what looked like electronic gloves to flip through screens on a clear panel set up in the control room. He frowned and spoke into his earpiece as he worked.

Jake waited until Mike noticed him before holding up Dani's laptop. "I need you to crack this and access the files."

Mike lowered his hands. "Whose is it? And why?"

"Everett's. She hacked into the company under our investigation. I need to know what she found."

Mike walked over and took the laptop. "She won't tell you?" he asked after a minute of tinkering with the password.

"No."

Mike stood up and looked at him. "And she still works here?"

His words left Jake cold as realization hit. This was ample cause for firing someone, if not incurring charges for breaking the law.

He wasn't sure why he cared what happened to the feisty Danielle Everett, but he did. Last night he'd thought for sure she'd tell him what she was doing. He knew it had to have something to do with her missing friend. She'd softened toward him and he knew from the desperate look in her eyes that she was in some kind of trouble. He'd seen that look too often in men under his command when they'd gotten in over their heads. Hopefully this wasn't a life-or-death situation.

He headed to Knight's office, since he was technically his commanding officer on this mission. Jake needed to let him know what was going on. Dani had proved last night that she was capable of lying to a co-worker and was an accomplished thief. She'd have probably done well in the

CIA.

His lips twitched as he remembered her defiance in the face of his anger last night. Once he'd seen those files, he'd lost his cool, something that rarely happened. But the thought that she could be messing with the mob and endangering herself made him lose control.

He stopped as he entered Knight's domain. He needed more information before he got her fired. Knight's receptionist, Ms. Waters, looked up from her book. "Can I help you?"

"No. I changed my mind."

She shrugged and went back to her novel.

Jake stood debating for a moment before clearing his throat. Ms. Waters turned a page and kept reading.

"I need information," he said.

She didn't look up, just turned a page. "Yes?"

"Personnel files."

She moved her book to the side and gave him a pitying look. "They're on the system, under personnel."

"I need more info."

"Koven. Fifth floor," she said, turning back to her book.

Jake walked away. Working with civilians might just be the end of his sanity.

He found Koven's office. Marc Koven, a CSIS agent, Canada's equivalent of the FBI and CIA rolled into one, was in charge of intel for this investigation. Apparently he also had access to personnel records that others didn't.

Jake rapped on the door and entered to find a man with

dark hair almost brushing his shoulders, which contrasted oddly with his khakis and crisp white dress shirt. He looked up from his laptop as Jake entered.

"I was told to see you. I need information on Everett from IT."

Koven leaned back in his chair. "You're Harrison, the new SEAL here to take us for a test ride, is that right?"

"Call me Jake. And I'm not posted here, if that's what you're asking."

Koven smiled. "It wasn't, but I've got my answer."

Jake wasn't sure how to take that, so he didn't reply. Koven looked laidback, but Jake had seen his record, or the parts of it that weren't classified. This guy was beyond smart.

"You want to know about Danielle Everett? Why don't you ask Chuck? He's the one who sponsored her to work here."

"Chuck might be a little biased."

Koven's lips twisted ruefully. "He might. What is it you need?" He started typing.

"Her psychological profile and a deep background check."

Koven tapped a few more keys and read something on his screen before studying Jake a moment, then he nodded. "Technically, her juvenile records are sealed, so I can't let you read them."

"But she has sealed records." Jake blew out a breath. That usually meant someone had been involved in criminal activity as a kid. Had she gotten a job at E.D.G.E. as a cover for her hacking? No. There was no way E.D.G.E. hadn't fully checked into her. They'd know if she was doing something illegal or not.

"Does her background have anything to do with the *Bratva*?"

Koven closed his laptop. "If you suspect she's done something, then she needs to be suspended pending investigation. If she hasn't done anything, then I'd like her for my team."

By not answering, Koven had basically confirmed Jake's suspicions. Had Dani worked for the mob as a kid? But more importantly, was she working for them again?

Dani knocked on Jake's door. He'd been here less than a week and he already had his own office and team, one that she hoped never to be on. Though she doubted she'd even have a job here after today.

"Come in," Jake said. He sat behind a desk that held nothing but a file and a laptop. An empty bookshelf was the only other thing in the office.

Dani strode in and stuck her thumbs through her belt loops. She wore tight, ripped jeans, an old Darth Vader t-shirt, leather wraps on her wrists, and rings in her upper ear. Her dark hair was caught up in a high ponytail. "I'm here, as ordered."

Jake's eyes widened slightly before his gaze traveled up and down her body. "I can see that."

Dani suppressed a shiver and stood tall, daring him to say anything. She was done with trying to be something she wasn't. And she wasn't a stuffy suit. If Jake or anyone at E.D.G.E. didn't like it then they could shove it.

She'd survive though. She always did.

"So, are you going to get me fired?" she asked.

Jake tilted his head as he watched her with those piercing eyes. "Should I, hacker girl?"

She gritted her teeth in annoyance. She hated playing games. "Just get it over with."

"Have a seat." He nodded to the chair in front of his desk.

She flopped into the seat and drew one booted foot up onto the chair. He looked at her foot and then at her. She compressed her lips and kept her foot up. She was acting like a sullen teen, but she couldn't seem to help it. Something about this man and this situation reduced her to a seething mass of emotions.

"Tell me why," Jake said.

Dani couldn't see any anger or condemnation in his face, but neither could she see compassion. "Does it matter?"

"I know this will surprise you, but it does to me." He studied her a moment and she fought against squirming.

"I'm guessing you've had a hard life," he said. "And that you've done your share of criminal deeds." He paused and took a breath. "But you found your way out. I understand how hard that is and I respect you for it. You're a fighter."

He paused as if waiting for her to say something, but she kept her mouth shut. Was this an act to see if she'd confess? He didn't fidget or keep talking, he just sat there calmly, like her job and life weren't on the line.

"If I tell you why, are you going to get me fired anyway?" she asked.

"Is keeping your job important to you?"

She snorted. "Only if I want to keep eating."

His eyes went icy. "So this place is only a paycheck to you?"

She sucked in a breath. "That's not what I meant." She put her foot on the floor and leaned forward. "I like it here. You're right, I haven't had a great life. This is the first job I've had where I respect myself. I want to work here. I want…"

He watched her closely. "What do you want?"

"I know this isn't just a security company. I think E.D.G.E. does a lot more than corporate security. All of the operators are military or CIA and CSIS, and I want to help. I want to do something good with my life, to help others. I want to be a field operator."

His voice matched his frost-laden eyes. "Then tell me the truth."

She hesitated for only a fraction of a second. He wasn't her supervisor, but she knew he could get her in deep trouble with a single complaint. But even more than that, she wanted him to understand her, to know she wasn't a criminal anymore. That she'd given up that life long ago.

"It started three nights ago when my friend went out on

a date…" She told him what had been happening and what she'd found. He listened intently and every now and then asked a pointed question, but otherwise he let her talk. When she was done he stared into space, a small frown furrowing his brow.

"You'd be willing to let us look over the information on your laptop?" he asked.

"Of cour—"

The door burst open and Chuck stomped in. "You leave her alone."

A tall, lean man with longish dark hair followed behind more sedately and shrugged his shoulders. "Sorry about the interruption, but Chuck felt someone might need a rescue."

Jake stood up. "Danielle, have you met Agent Koven? He's from CSIS."

Dani stood, wary of what he was doing here, and extended her hand to shake Koven's. "Call me Dani," she said.

He nodded. "I'm Marc." He lifted her laptop. "Mike gave this to me. Pretty interesting stuff on here. Do you speak Russian?"

Dani swallowed and her gaze flitted to Chuck, who gave a slight nod. "Yes, though I'm a bit rusty."

Koven gave her a quick perusal up and down, his gaze calculating. "I could definitely use someone like you on my team, if you're interested."

"No, thanks," she said. "First I need to know exactly what E.D.G.E. is and what your team would do. It's past time someone told me who you guys really are."

Koven's eyebrows rose but he didn't say anything, just nodded and handed her laptop back.

Chuck squared his shoulders. "I think we should take this little gathering up to Knight's office. He can explain everything."

"I agree," said Jake. "Also, Dani's found out some useful information pertinent to this op. Knight should hear it."

Dani suppressed a smile at the look of consternation on her old friend's face. He'd obviously come in here expecting to defend her. She gave him a small smile and a nod, trying to act confident about the way things were turning out, even though her stomach roiled at the thought of what they might ask her to do.

"I'll get Blackwell too," Koven said. "He's back from an overseas mission and needs to be brought up to speed."

Before they trooped out of the office, Chuck put a hand on her shoulder and squeezed. "I'm sorry I didn't believe you about your friend."

She laid her hand over his, very aware that Jake stood a few feet away watching intently. "There was no evidence to back me up," she said. "Of course you wouldn't believe me."

Chuck pressed his lips together. "But that's just it. I shouldn't need evidence when you're the one telling me."

Dani didn't know what to do with that admission. She'd always had to prove herself. It seemed strange that anyone would just take her word on something. Her thumb rubbed the small scar on her shoulder. It had been given to her by

Vladimir when he'd thought she'd been lying to him.

She lifted her gaze and met Jake's intense one, as if he were trying to see inside her. She dropped her hand and forced a smile for Chuck. "You're an old cop," she said. "Of course you need evidence."

When Dani walked into Knight's office, Derrick Blackwell waited for them. Introduced as Knight's second-in-command, he sprawled his long, muscled body on one of the comfy chairs in the corner. He looked as though he was about to fall asleep, but his slitted eyes gave her the impression of a resting lion, ready to pounce.

His dark hair had a few streaks of gray at the temples, but otherwise he looked younger than his late thirties. According to Ashley, he'd asked her out on a date. Looking at him now, she seriously doubted he even knew who Ashley was.

Rhys, Mike, and the female operator with the cold eyes came into the room as well. When everyone had assembled around the conference table, Knight looked at Dani. "E.D.G.E. is the Elite Digital and Global Enforcement for International Security. We are a secret organization connected to, and yet separate from, our governments. We can go where governments can't. We can get the job done faster because we have no red tape to cut through."

"Governments," Dani said. "Are there more than just Canada and the United States represented by E.D.G.E.?"

Knight smiled. "That is above your pay grade. You know more than you should at this point, but we're forced to trust you with this mission. It's time for you to tell us what you know."

And so Dani went through everything she knew about Tassia's disappearance again.

No one asked questions, though Agent Koven typed on his laptop while she spoke. When she finished, she crossed her arms. "So will you help me find her?"

Knight exchanged a glance with Blackwell, then he looked at Jake, and Dani suppressed a groan. They wanted to keep her out of the loop. "Look," she said, "I can help."

"We appreciate your offer, Dani," Knight said, leaning back in his chair. "But I want to know if you've told us everything that might be pertinent to this operation."

His gaze held her and she wanted to squirm. Should she tell them about her past? Was it really necessary for them to know *everything*?

"I think we should use her," Koven said. "She speaks Russian and she's got experience. She's an asset."

The skin on Dani's scalp prickled with unease at Koven's choice of words.

Jake held up his hands. "No. She's untrained. I'm not having her endanger my team."

Dani scowled. So much for him being on her side. Did he really think she'd mess everything up? "My friend has been kidnapped. I'm going to do everything in my power to get her back."

With or without you, she thought.

"This is an op already in progress," Jake said. "You're completely untrained, Danielle. You'd be a hindrance. No offense."

She arched an eyebrow. "Offense taken," she said. "You know nothing about me or what I can do."

Koven held up a finger. "Actually, she *is* trained in this. And I say we need her."

Dani's sliver of satisfaction dwindled at the look of intense calculation in Koven's eyes. He'd obviously read her juvie file, the one that should have been sealed. At least he didn't know *all* the sordid details—those, only she and Chuck knew.

"I've been after the Rusakov family for years," he said. "They have an international reach and connections to terrorist groups. You could help us take them down."

Dani stiffened. No one betrayed the Rusakov family and lived.

"You know them," Jake said. He must have noticed her reaction.

She swallowed. "I ran into them when I was young."

All of them stared at her as if they knew there was a lot more to the story. But it was a story she wouldn't share.

"Then you're lucky to be alive today," Jake said quietly.

"Why'd they take Tassia?" Dani clenched her fists, praying it wasn't because of her.

Knight tapped a file in front of him. "The Public Prosecutor was looking into the Volga Group for tax evasion. I think they suspected something more than that, but couldn't prove anything. Tassia was helping with the case and had access to all the information."

"Dammit," Dani said, and straightened. "Her laptop and all the files from her desk are missing." She swallowed against a dry throat. What else had they discovered? Did they realize who Tassia's neighbor was?

"They want to know what the Public Prosecutor knows," Knight said. "And your friend was the easiest way to get that intel."

"Do you… Do you think she's still alive?" Dani asked.

Knight didn't look away, but the lines on his forehead deepened. "We're working under the assumption that she is."

Her stomach clenched as she imagined what must be happening to Tassia. "What's the next step?"

"The Rusakovs are having a party," Koven said with a smile that Dani didn't trust. "And Danielle's invited herself."

Chuck stood up. "Dani, no. What if they recognize you?"

"I've changed an awful lot from the kid I once was," she said.

He shook his head. "Not enough."

"She won't be going in alone," Jake said.

"I'll be your date," Koven said.

Jake's head snapped toward the other man. "*No. I'll* be her date."

"You may be a SEAL," Koven replied in an even tone, "but you don't know undercover work."

"I've done my share of undercover, and besides, I'm trained to know what to do when the shit hits the fan. I'm the best choice and you know it."

Koven's eyes narrowed. "You don't—"

"Agent Koven," Knight said quietly. "Lieutenant Harrison will be going in with Ms. Everett. You and Petty Officer Lafayette will be their backup."

"Yes, sir," Koven bit out.

Dani could tell that Agent Koven thought of the Rusakov family as his case and he didn't want to give up the lead. She didn't trust Koven to have her back, but she wasn't sure if Jake was a better choice. She wasn't sure he trusted her fully. Would he let her do what needed to be done? Or would he just try to protect her?

She pressed her lips together and stood up to leave the room. It really didn't matter who her partner was. She'd end up looking after herself like she always did.

CHAPTER 8

J ake sat behind the wheel of a borrowed black Ferarri parked in the Golden Mile district, an exclusive neighborhood of Montreal.

The target's house was on Redpath Crescent, right below the park the other operators referred to as the Mountain. He spoke aloud. "Zero, this is Alpha. Radio check, over."

"Reading you five by five, Alpha." Rhys's voice spoke through the tiny receiver inserted into his left ear. The equally tiny but powerful microphone lay under a small layer of fake skin by his collarbone, under his new dress shirt. He pulled at the collar.

"So how come you get to do all the fun things while I have to sit in a van with a spook?" Rhys asked, his drawl more pronounced. He must be ribbing Koven about something.

And sure enough, Koven grumbled in the background.

Jake scanned the high-end street. Few pedestrians, and light traffic. The party was two blocks down. The dark van where Rhys and Koven sat was another block behind him. "I wouldn't call dressing in a monkey suit fun."

"You haven't seen your partner yet," Rhys said. "I'll trade you."

Jake's jaw clenched. "I was assigned to this op."

"Buddy, you volunteered. Not that I blame you."

"She needed decent backup," he said.

Rhys laughed. "You should see the spook's face right now. By the way, she's coming up on your six."

Jake looked in the rearview mirror and saw a silhouetted figure walking toward the car. He sucked in a breath.

Her dress was black, long, and had a high slit that showed a shapely leg with every other step. She had a white wrap around her shoulders, so he couldn't see the top of her dress.

She stopped at the car and he saw her tighten her grip on her wrap before she pulled open the Ferarri's door. She slid in, exposing one leg all the way to the thigh.

His mouth went dry at the sight and he forced his gaze away. Her hair was piled on top of her head in an elegant way, and held in place with some sticks. It looked as if all you had to do was pull them out and all that dark silkiness would tumble down her back. His fingers itched to do just that.

He needed to get a grip.

"You look…nice," he said.

Her gaze went to his, and her tongue darted out to touch her upper lip. A lick of flame curled through him. She stilled, watching him like prey scenting danger, before looking away. He made her nervous.

"Thank you," she said, responding to his compliment.

He nodded, suddenly aware that everything they said was being picked up by his mic. He pushed his emotions away. Game time. "You ready for this?" he asked.

She nodded and rolled her shoulders under her wrap.

"Then let's do it." He put the car in gear and pulled out onto the street.

"Zero, on way to location now."

"Roger that, Alpha."

"Do they hear me too? Should I do a radio check?" Dani asked. She gripped a small black purse in her hands.

"Zero, does Bravo have comms?" The houses around them grew bigger and farther apart. Within moments the target was in sight.

"Affirmative, Alpha."

"Can you hear me, Rhys?" Dani asked.

"No names," Jake told her, pulling into the circular drive of an upscale stone mansion complete with classic pillars. Luxury cars parked on the driveway ahead of him. He could see valets helping passengers out and slipping into the drivers' seats.

"Five by five, chère," Rhys said.

"Keep it professional, Lucky," Jake said, and then ground

his teeth when he heard his buddy snort.

"Relax, College. I've got your six."

"And mine?" Dani asked.

"We all do," Jake said before Rhys could answer. "We're at location. Alpha out." Jake pulled up in front of the wide steps leading to double doors. A valet in a dark short coat came to his door.

Jake turned to Dani. Her wide eyes stared into his. Damn, he hated bringing her into this. He squeezed her hand. "Stick close to me and you'll be fine."

She took a deep breath and took her hand back. "I don't need your protection, Jake." She opened her door and let the valet take her hand before he could respond.

Jake stepped out and came around to Dani. She looked elegant and perfectly composed. He still didn't want her out of his sight.

They walked up the steps, approaching an older gentleman in a tux waiting at the doors. "Name?" he asked in a heavy Russian accent.

"D. Everett and guest," Jake said. The man checked his list and then waved them inside.

The foyer had a winding staircase on one side and a massive crystal chandelier that threw sparkles of light on the marble floor.

Double doors opened into an actual ballroom where men in tuxes and women in jewels sipped champagne under the glittering light of more chandeliers. Classical music overlaid the chatter of the guests, while waiters carrying platters of hors d'oeuvres and trays of drinks roamed the floor.

He was so out of his element. Give him an assault rifle and some tangos to take care of any day. Maybe Koven should have been the one in the monkey suit after all.

A servant offered to take Dani's wrap. She dropped it off her shoulders and into the woman's waiting hands.

Jake's gut clenched and he forgot the party. Her black dress had a deep V in both front and back, revealing the creamy, smooth skin between her silk-covered breasts. He stepped toward her, wanting to trace the edge of the V that passed over the swell of her breast. She stepped back, her eyes wide.

He needed to get control and fast. He forced a smile and held out his arm. She curled her fingers around it, but managed to keep as much space between their bodies as possible.

Using her arm, he pulled her closer and leaned in, breathing in the scent of vanilla, citrus, and woman, before whispering in her ear so softly the sensitive microphone wouldn't pick it up. "I'm your date and lover for the evening. You must look like a woman who enjoys my touch."

A blush rose in her cheeks and she looked away. This wouldn't do. He captured her chin in his hand and forced her gaze back to his. Her breathing hitched as he stroked one finger along her jaw. Her eyes stared into his as his finger moved down her neck. He wasn't sure what possessed him. He knew what he was doing wasn't professional, but he had to touch her, to see if her skin was as silky as her dress.

It was. His finger traced along her collarbone before starting to follow the plunging V of her dress. She shivered, her eyes darkening.

He wanted more. He leaned in, his finger still trailing down her hot skin.

"Alpha, Bravo, are you in position?"

Jake stiffened and grabbed her hand on his arm before she could jerk away. He leaned closer to her and smiled as if they shared a secret. "In position, Zero, wait out."

Dani's lips parted as she took a deep breath, drawing Jake's eyes down to the black fabric that covered her breasts. He wanted to shove the material aside and lay her bare. He swallowed. Now was not the time.

Soon, Jake promised himself. She was trouble, but he might need a bit of trouble in his life to spice up his trip to Canada.

He slid his arm around her waist and nodded toward the ballroom. "Shall we?"

What the hell just happened?

Dani surfaced from the swirling desire and looked around. No one seemed to be aware of them. Couples dressed in gowns, jewels, and tuxedos loitered around the foyer or entered the ballroom. Jake stood composed and patient, as if he hadn't just created a whirlwind of sensation inside her, ensnaring her in a vortex of heat without her consent.

Why had he touched her like that? Just to make it seem as though they were a couple in lust? She grit her teeth, wishing she hadn't fallen for it.

His gray eyes met hers. "Let's rock and roll."

He was right. It was time to work. She took in a deep, calming breath and released it. Jake's gaze darted down to her chest for an instant before meeting hers again. Heat flickered in his eyes before he banked it.

So he hadn't been just acting a part. Something about knowing he'd been as affected as she had made her bold. Two could play at this game.

She smiled, leaned close, and placed a hand on his chest, before putting her lips close to his neck. He froze, but otherwise didn't react. "I'm ready when you are." Her breath whispered along his skin. His arm tightened around her waist briefly before she pulled back.

His eyes narrowed. She arched a brow at him. It was time he learned she could hold her own. He nodded and slid his hand down until it rested against the bare skin of her lower back.

She worked to keep her smile composed and her mind focused as they entered the room, knowing that would be much easier if she didn't have a large muscled man trailing his fingers almost absentmindedly up and down the skin of her lower back. She used the excuse of grabbing a champagne flute from a passing waiter to step away from him.

Dani scanned the crowd while she calmed her heart. It was quite the party. At least a hundred people mingled in the room. She heard snatches of conversation in Russian, English, and French. There were almost enough people present that she felt hidden from the Rusakovs, though far from safe.

Floor-to-ceiling windows occupied the front of the room, framed by heavy silk drapes that pooled on the floor. The crush of people hid most of the back of the room. But she did see some closed French doors and a swinging door that waiters moved in and out of.

Dani's heels clicked on the highly polished floor as they moved farther into the room.

"Do you see anyone?" Jake asked.

Agent Koven had shown them updated photos of Dmitri and Vladimir Rusakov and their known henchmen. Dmitri hadn't changed much, just a bit more silver at his temples.

"No," she said. "You?"

"Negative." He held out his arm. "Let's mingle."

She took his arm and felt the muscles beneath his tux. She'd seen some of the weapons he'd planned on bringing tonight and wondered where he'd hidden them all. He was an incredibly dangerous man, and no one knew it but her.

Well, maybe not. Jake looked amazing in a tux, the jacket defining his broad shoulders and narrow waist. He moved with an athlete's grace through the crowd. Confidence and danger emanated from him like an aura and it attracted attention. Mostly female attention.

Dani felt the eyes on them, even if Jake didn't. They weren't the gazes of an enemy, but still, they stalked him. The women who glanced their way took second and third glances. A few openly stared, sensual avarice highlighting their faces. Dani glared at one woman whose breasts looked as if they were about to pop out of her dress. The woman just shrugged at Dani and kept watching.

Jake stopped them by the far wall, which held a marble fireplace. No fire burned, but some designer had laid out perfectly cut logs. From this position they could watch both entrances and their backs were protected by the wall.

"This was a bad idea," Dani muttered.

"What?" Jake asked. "You coming here? Do you want to abort?"

Dani suppressed her eye roll. "You won't be able to move without half the people here tracking you."

He stiffened slightly. "What do you mean?"

"Seriously?" She tilted her head back the way they'd come. "Look at the women, Jake."

He did another slow scan of the crowd, and this time multiple women caught his eye and smiled their invitations. He cleared his throat and faced her.

"Are you blushing?" Dani asked. She covered her mouth to stop the laugh that threatened to escape.

Jake pulled his shoulders back. "No." He shifted his stance and went back to surveying the crowd. His lips twisted. "You're right. It's going to be difficult to slip out of this room."

"I can do it."

"Not on your own," Jake said without a trace of humor in his voice.

"It makes the most sense, Jake. I'm your partner. Trust me."

"You're my *untrained* partner," Jake muttered.

She forced a smile. "You're the one who wanted to come with me. So stop complaining." She waited a moment. "And could you smile a bit? We're attracting attention. It looks like we're having a fight and some of those women are salivating."

He smiled at her and nodded, playing his part, his gaze continuing to roam the crowd, scanning for threats. He placed his hand on the small of her back again, causing her to shiver.

"Cold?" he asked.

She shook her head and smoothed her dress down. She had to take care of it, since she'd borrowed it from Tass.

"So when did you learn Russian?" Jake asked.

"My father was Russian. I learned as a child." She smiled and watched the crowd, but she could feel his scrutiny.

"Your last name isn't Russian," he observed.

"My last name is different than when I was a child." She decided to change the topic. "How long have you been... doing what you're doing?"

"Eight years," he said. "How'd you meet Chuck?" he asked, apparently undeterred by her topic change.

"What is this? Get-to-know-Dani night?"

His lips twitched. A waiter passed them carrying a tray of food and he snagged two tiny shrimp skewers. He offered one to her. "We have to pass the time somehow."

She took the shrimp. It smelled of garlic and something spicy. Her stomach rumbled. "We're not here to enjoy ourselves." She ate the shrimp in two bites. She'd been too nervous to eat much dinner.

Jake motioned to another waiter and took a napkin and loaded it with bits of steak, shrimp, and a fancy cracker dabbed with creamy cheese and chopped peppers. He avoided the caviar. He held out the napkin to her, his eyes serious. "Eat while you can."

She wanted to glare at him, but her stomach rumbled again. She selected the bit of skewered steak and tried not to moan in appreciation at the flavor. Jake nodded his approval and her lips quirked.

She'd almost finished the selection when Jake stilled, eyes on the front of the room. The chiming of a bell drew everyone else's attention to what he'd already noticed.

Dmitri Rusakov stood between two of the large windows at the front of the room, holding a champagne glass and smiling. The waiter with the bell withdrew to the edge of the room.

"My favored guests," Dmitri said. "I appreciate you all coming to my humble gathering. We are here to celebrate my son's return from Russia. It's been a long five years, but he has achieved much in that time."

He turned to the main entrance, swept out an arm, and

Vladimir strode over to take his position beside his father. Dani stopped breathing, her body paralyzed as she saw the tall, magnetically handsome man who still featured prominently in her nightmares. She couldn't hear Dmitri's speech past the buzzing in her ears.

She became aware of Jake's arm around her, holding her close, his mouth at her ear whispering her name. Warmth seeped back into her and she pulled away slightly to meet his eyes.

"You scared me," he whispered, continuing to hold her tight. "You don't have to do this, Dani."

"I do if I want to find Tassia," she said, pleased that her voice came out calm and even.

A muscle jumped in his jaw. "Fine," he said. "Remember, I've got your back."

She nodded, and actually believed him. It was a nice feeling to know she wasn't alone. She didn't move away from his arm and Jake didn't take it away. After a moment, she could feel her heartbeat steadying. If it thumped a little harder than usual, that was understandable.

"I implore you all to partake of the food and drink," Dmitri was saying. "This is an evening for fun. *Santé.*" He raised his glass.

The partygoers all raised their glasses and echoed the toast to their health. Everyone watched Dmitri and Vladimir. Jake scanned the area.

"I'm going to slip away now," Dani whispered.

Jake looked at her sharply. "Alone?"

Dani nodded and discreetly touched her ear. "I'll let you know if I need anything. I'm just a woman who's had too much champagne and needs a quiet moment."

Jake grabbed her arm before she could move. "Be careful. Keep us in the loop. If anything happens, anything at all, then use the safe word and I'll come for you."

Dani's nerves evened out. She nodded and smiled widely for anyone watching. "I'll be fine."

CHAPTER 9

With all eyes still on Dmitri and Vladimir at the front of the room, Dani made her way to the swinging door the waiters used, carrying her still-full champagne glass.

She stepped into a formal dining room with a door at the other end that, based on the smells and sounds, led to the kitchen. The room was stately, with a long, polished mahogany table and a dozen chairs around it. A Persian carpet done in reds and blues protected the floor, while oil paintings of landscapes adorned the walls.

Near the kitchen entrance was an open door leading to a hallway. She aimed for it. The plush carpet muffled her steps and she walked with a slight sway, champagne held high as if she were concentrating on not spilling it.

Hopefully she could pull off a tipsy lady, even though her nerves were edged like swords.

The team back at E.D.G.E. had found the builder's plans for Dmitri's house, and she knew from them that there was an office on the first floor. But the plans had also shown a smaller room with ethernet connections near the master suite upstairs.

That was Dmitri's personal office, and where she was headed now. She'd never make it up the grand stairs in the front of the house without discovery, which was why she was heading for the servant stairs in the back.

A petite blonde waitress, her ponytail swinging with each step, came out of the kitchen carrying a tray laden with food. "Excuse me, miss. Can I help you?"

"Where is the washroom?" Dani asked in Russian.

The woman's eyes widened uncertainly.

Dani pointed to the hall she wanted. "Bathroom," she said in a heavy accent and moved past the waitress, adding just a bit more sway to her step.

As she suspected, the woman didn't say anything more and kept on with her job. No one wanted to interfere with a drunk Russian. Especially one who seemed to know where she was going and therefore must have been a guest at some point.

Dani moved into the hallway and ahead of her was a narrow staircase leading up. Her heart began to pound harder.

"At the stairs," she said quietly, knowing the mic tucked

into her bodice would pick up her words. Jake and the others would know where she was.

"Copy," Jake's voice said in her tiny earpiece.

Her heart slowed a bit at hearing his voice. She wasn't in this alone. It was an unusual feeling for her.

One she shouldn't get used to.

A quick glance showed an empty hall and she darted up the steps, her heels sinking into the carpet. She wished she could have worn her boots. Running and fighting would be severely hampered by the stilettos, but her Doc Martens just didn't cut it with the slinky dress she'd borrowed from Tassia.

The stairs opened onto another hallway with plush gray carpeting, creamy walls, and closed doors. According to the plans, the second door on the left was the master bedroom overlooking the back gardens. The next door should be the office.

Her breathing was too fast as she put her ear to it and listened for a moment. Nothing. She slowly twisted the knob. It stopped. Locked.

"Zero. Outside location." She'd remembered not to say any names.

"Copy, Bravo, over." Rhys's friendly drawl echoed in her ear. She found she missed Jake's low, curt tones.

She set her champagne down on the floor and pulled two pins from the hair piled on her head.

She'd specially designed these lock picks as a teen. She inserted them into the keyhole and jiggled them until she felt the tumblers. Twisting the picks together, the knob turned and the lock sprang open.

She opened the door and peeked inside. Dark, except for the moonlight streaming through the windows, highlighting the large desk. Bookshelves covered one wall, opposite the closed door leading to the master suite. A small couch and coffee table completed the room's layout.

Dani grabbed her champagne and closed the door behind her, slipping the picks back into her hair. She set her flute glass on the desk, sat in the chair, and pulled the keyboard toward her.

The monitor came to life, asking for a password. From her clutch, she pulled out a mini version of her hacking program. It was amazing the technology E.D.G.E. could get their hands on. She'd modified the program last night and hoped it and her code could crack the password in minutes.

She attached it to the USB port of the hard drive and tapped a few keys on her device. She set it on the desk and waited for it to do its magic.

"Zero, I'm waiting for the shell to crack."

"Copy, Bravo, over."

Again it was Rhys's voice. Why wasn't Jake answering like the first time? Was he okay? Should she ask?

The blue computer screen in front of her dissolved into a normal PC desktop. A picture of a Siberian tiger floated in the background, its piercing blue eyes cold and predatory.

She wiped her damp palms on her dress. "Sorry, Tass," she muttered and started typing.

"Say again, Bravo, over."

"Oh. Nothing to worry about, Zero. Just talking to myself."

"Protocol, Bravo." That was Koven. Her lips twisted.

"I'm working," she said. "Don't annoy me."

A soft snort came over the line and she knew it was Jake. He was okay. She smiled as she started to scan the files on Dmitri's computer. She stuck a flash drive in the system and started copying everything she thought might be relevant. Some of it was in English and some in Russian. He must have a Cyrillic keyboard somewhere.

"The shell is cracked and spilling the goods now. Should be done in a few minutes," Dani said.

Koven sighed and Dani smirked. So what if she didn't have great radio protocol? She could do this. She could be an operator or a spy or whatever they all were.

A door closed. Voices spoke in Russian. Her blood iced in her veins. The voices were coming from the bedroom next door. It had to be Dmitri.

"There's someone next door," she whispered. "I think it's Dmitri."

"Exfil to extraction location, Bravo," Rhys said in a calm and too-even voice.

"On my way, Bravo," Jake said.

She swept her hacking device into her clutch and hesitated over pulling the flash drive from the computer. She hadn't gotten all the files. What if she missed something that would help find Tassia?

The voices next door rose in an argument. One was female. A slap sounded.

Dani's blood fired at the thought of a woman being beaten, but she couldn't help her. "Come on," she whispered.

"Bravo, sitrep," Rhys said.

The voices were quieter now, but the male's was no less harsh.

"Eighty-five percent," Dani whispered.

"Exfil means get out," Jake's voice said in her ear. "Now."

"I know what it means," Dani said.

"*Shit*. Wait out," Jake said. A small grunt sounded through the earpiece.

"Get out, Bravo," Rhys's voice said, still calm.

A small window popped up on the computer screen. *File transfer complete*. She removed the flash drive, closed the open windows, and clicked off the monitor.

She couldn't hear anything from next door. She hurried to the door, tucking the flash drive into her bra just in case she lost her purse.

She looked back as she started to turn the knob. Her champagne glass rested on the desk. Dammit.

She sprinted across the room and grabbed it. Back at the door, she listened carefully before she cracked it open. The hallway was empty.

She moved out, closing and locking the door behind her, breathing out slowly. She strode to the small set of stairs and realized a burly man in a black suit stood facing down the steps. She paused and cursed silently. He must be one of Dmitri's bodyguards.

She turned to go down the main stairs. Maybe she could get down those unnoticed.

"Stop." The heavy Russian accent made the low voice seem deeper and more commanding. She stumbled and spilled a bit of her champagne.

"Yessh?" She whirled, her arms too wide, spilling more champagne and smiling broadly at the approaching guard.

"What are you doing here? You are not allowed up here." He grabbed her arm and gave it a little shake. She let her head rock with the small movement.

"Stop that," she said, still trying to slur her words, swatting at him ineffectively with her clutch. "I was looking for my husband. I know he's off with that nasty blonde woman. He's here somewhere." She looked mournfully at her glass of champagne, now mostly spilled because of the arm shaking. "Could you be a dear and get me another?"

The guard growled something low and full of Russian curses before shoving her toward the kitchen stairs. "Your husband is not up here. Go home now or I will see that you never get home."

She let her eyes widen in fear and squeaked as she wobbled her way to the steps. Once there, she raced down, growing steadier as she went. She chanced a look back to make sure the guard hadn't followed her.

Strong arms snagged her and pulled her against a hard body. She dropped her champagne glass and struck backward with her elbow. A grunt sounded before Jake's voice growled in her ear. "Relax. It's me."

She didn't relax, but jerked away from him. "What the hell are you doing? Trying to freak me out?"

"Alpha, sitrep, over."

Dani answered instead. "I have it. We're leaving." She turned to the front of the house and strode down the hallway. Jake grabbed her hand.

"Not that way," he said, tugging her toward the back of the house.

"What did you do?" she asked.

"One of Dmitri's guards got in my way," Jake said. "I took care of him, but I didn't have time to hide him well."

A scream sounded from the front of the house.

Jake sighed. "I had to stick him in the ladies."

Dani struggled not to smile at his disgruntlement. "Do you have an exit plan?"

Jake still hadn't released her hand as they walked calmly through the kitchen. "The back door," he said.

One of the chefs looked up from plating appetizers and scowled at them. Dani smiled apologetically at her. "Loved the food."

Jake snorted and pulled her from the kitchen into a room that looked like a cross between a mudroom and a storage room. Through the glass back door, she could see a garage where a truck with a catering logo sat parked. This entryway must be for the servants.

Jake put his hand on the doorknob and looked at her. "You did good up there, hacker girl, thinking on your feet like that."

Warmth spilled through her. "Thanks," she said. "And thanks for coming for me."

He smiled. "You didn't need me. And for that, I'm impressed."

His gaze flicked beyond her, and he quickly let go of the door and pulled her fiercely into his arms. His mouth descended on hers. The warmth inside her turned to heat before surging into an inferno and whipping like wildfire through her. Her pulse pounded in her ears as his soft lips molded to hers. His tongue licked at her lips and her mouth opened, allowing him entrance. Her tongue darted out to touch his and waves of heat washed over her.

He groaned and his arms tightened around her before he whirled and pressed her back against the door. His hands roamed her body, not quite touching what needed to be touched. She pressed against him, all rational thought gone. He broke the kiss to trail his hot mouth up to her ear. Her hands clutched at his shoulders as sparks arced from her ear to the heat in her belly.

She moaned.

"Is he still there?" Jake's breathy whisper on the sensitive skin of her ear caused her to shudder. "Dani, is the guard still there?" Jake's fingers dug into her ribs and her eyes popped open.

A lean man in a black suit stood talking to the chef.

Dani closed her eyes and wanted to curl up inside of herself, far away from Jake and his fiery kiss. "Yes," she choked out, embarrassment tightening her throat.

The kiss hadn't been real, just a way to keep their cover. She prayed for the guard to leave so she could get out of there and away from Jake.

But she had to keep letting him nuzzle her neck. And *merde*, he was good at it. She couldn't control her shiver as he pressed his lips to her pounding pulse.

She kept her hands on his shoulders, though she really wanted to curl them into fists to help her stop the waves of sensation assaulting her body. Jake must have sensed something because he raised his face and stared into her eyes, so close that their breath mingled.

She couldn't move, couldn't look away from the heat and predatory gleam in his eyes. His gaze seared her, inside and out.

Jake blinked and the soldier took control, his gaze cooling and becoming assessing. "What's he doing now?"

She realized Jake had switched their positions so his broad back now protected her from the man, but she could see his frustration at not knowing what was happening behind him.

She leaned her forehead to his, pretending to want his attention. "He's finished talking with the chef." She watched for a second more. "He's in the hall. His back is to us."

Jake glanced back, nodded, and they slipped through the door. "Can you run in those?" he pointed to her spike heels.

She slipped them off and held them. "Let's go."

CHAPTER 10

J ake pulled his Sig Sauer P226 from the holster at his
lower back and moved silently along the back of the
house. His leg throbbed. The guard had managed to
kick it before Jake took him down. Now each step sent fire
burning through the limb.

Dani followed behind him, quiet. She'd obviously spent
time learning to be stealthy, and it only emphasized her
mysterious, and no doubt criminal, background.

He grit his teeth. The question was, was she *still* a
criminal? Could he trust her?

He scanned the dark lawn and the woods starting
twenty-five yards away. They'd have to run for it. His back
itched at the thought of being out in the open for that long,
but there was no hope for it. They had to move. It wouldn't

be long before the guards realized the kissing couple from the kitchen had disappeared.

The thought of that kiss sent heat racing through him and made his cock twitch. He could still feel Dani's body pressed against him, her hot lips under his, and hear the small moan that set his blood racing.

He blew out a breath. Now was not the time. He forced all thoughts of the kiss out of his head. He needed to focus and get them to the extraction site before they were discovered.

"Our people are through the woods and across a small stream." He glanced at her bare feet. They were going to get torn to shreds. Why hadn't anyone thought of that problem in the briefing? More importantly, why hadn't Dani brought it up?

He shrugged it off. He'd carry her if he had to, even with his crappy leg. He wouldn't leave her unprotected.

With a last glance around, he grabbed her hand and tugged her forward, starting to run. His leg protested each footfall, but he shoved it aside. Dani depended on him.

She kept up with him easily, so he increased his pace. Her stride lengthened and he felt a strange pride that she could match him.

They slowed to enter the woods, and bark splintered on a tree near his head. Dani stopped to look, but he dragged her into the darkness.

"Someone's shooting at us," he told her. Another crack and more bark exploded nearby.

Shouts came from the lawn. Too close. He wished for a

pair of NVGs, but he'd done enough training in the dark to have decent night vision without the goggles. He pulled Dani through the woods, ducking branches, jumping rotten logs, pushing both of them hard. Trying to stay quiet, but not reducing their speed.

The guards behind them continued to shout directions at each other in Russian, nicely giving away their locations to him. The stream was just yards in front of them. He slowed, his senses on high alert as he listened and scanned the open area ahead of them. The trees had been cleared on the other side of the stream and a six-foot concrete wall stood between them and the street where Rhys and Koven waited.

"I'll go and make sure it's clear," he whispered to Dani. "Then you run to me and I'll help you over."

Her jaw set. "Like hell. We'll both go and get over that wall right now." And she took off, leaping the stream and racing for the wall. He caught up easily, but stayed a step behind just in case she needed help.

She threw her shoes over the wall as she ran at it. Her hands gripped the top as she planted a foot on the wall and pushed off, going up and over, her long legs flashing pale through the slit in her dress.

He hadn't seen anything much sexier than that in his life. She kept a low profile as she slid over the wall, making sure her silhouette didn't stand out against the night sky.

He followed suit, but when he landed his leg crumpled under him and he stumbled.

"You okay?" she whispered.

"I'm fine." Damn his leg. The muscle around the injury threatened to cramp. He rubbed his hand along it, digging hard into the screaming muscles. She watched him and opened her mouth.

He cut her off, but kept his voice low. "I'm fine."

She huffed a breath. "Whatever." She picked up her shoes and took off at a jog.

He grit his teeth, but kept up with her. "By the way, nice work getting over the wall," he said, still speaking softly.

She curled her lip at him. "Do you underestimate every woman you're with?" She increased her pace.

What? He caught up with her again. His hand squeezed his thigh muscles as he ran, trying to stop the oncoming spasm. "Can't you take a compliment?"

She kept jogging toward the van containing their team just ahead. "Oh. Was that a compliment? It felt more like a pat on the head." She demonstrated with a hand gesture. "Good doggie."

He let her race ahead. What the hell? Why was she so ticked? He shook his head and continued to the van, rubbing at his leg. The threat of a cramp receded, thankfully. They piled into the van and took off, driving back to E.D.G.E. HQ where they'd debrief.

He sat quietly in the van while Dani pointedly ignored him. First her kiss made him burn and then she turned into an ice queen when he complimented her? She made no sense. He definitely needed to stay clear of Dani Everett.

Dani still wore Tassia's slinky dress an hour later when the debrief at E.D.G.E. finished. They sat at one end of a conference table in a room with multiple monitors on the wall. Mike sat at the other end, laptop open and going through the files Dani had taken from Dmitri's computer.

She, Jake, Rhys, and Koven filled in the stern-looking Blackwell on every little detail of the operation. Somehow they'd avoided all mention of the kiss. For which she was truly grateful.

She should feel elated about having completed a successful mission and shown everyone she could be a field operator, but instead she just felt exhausted.

Her eyes were gritty and she wanted to slump in her chair. Her feet throbbed from her run over rocks and forest debris. She'd shoved them back into her heels in the van. Right now, the sole of her left foot had its own heartbeat and warmth trickled down between her toes. She figured she'd stepped on glass or a sharp rock.

"Have you gotten anything useful yet, Mike?" Blackwell asked the IT guru.

"Not yet, sir. Some of the files are in Russian. I think I could use Dani's help with this."

Dani wanted to groan. She just wanted a shower and her bed.

But Tassia had been in the Rusakovs' hands for five days now.

"Pass it here," she said.

Mike slid his laptop down to her. "I've highlighted the files that I think might be useful. Let me know what you think."

The others continued to talk while she started to delve into the system. Her mind awoke at the puzzle before her. But that had always been the case. Anytime she had an interesting hack, she'd stay awake late into the night until she cracked it. She slid her shoes off and the distracting throbbing eased.

She started going through the files Mike had suggested first. Something wasn't quite right. She started coordinating emails with the spreadsheets tracking shipments.

"I think I've got something," she said, looking up. Only Jake was left in the room. "Where'd everyone go?"

"Home," he said. Then he smiled. "Actually, I think Mike is bunking in the ops room. I don't know if that guy ever goes home."

She looked at her watch. Three in the morning. She'd been going over this for an hour. "You waited for me?"

"You're my partner. We watch each other's backs."

She froze for a moment. Those simple words struck her hard. Had she ever had anyone watch her back before? Jake's gaze seemed to dig into her soul, unwilling to accept the surface facade that no one else bothered to look beyond.

She ducked her head to get away from those piercing eyes. She needed to get a handle on herself. He was just sitting at a table, probably only because he had to. It didn't mean anything. She took a deep breath and exhaled slowly before looking up.

Jake's head tilted as he studied her. "You haven't had many partners, have you?"

Her cheeks warmed. What was he trying to do to her? She set her jaw. It didn't matter. Only Tassia mattered right now. "Do you want to hear what I found or not?"

He shook his head. "Damn, you're tough."

"Is that a compliment?"

He laughed. "Shit. Just show me what you found, hacker girl."

His laugh eased around her like her favorite pair of cozy pajamas. Her muscles relaxed and she smiled as she twisted the laptop so he could see the screen. "As far as I can tell, Dmitri has a legitimate import business dealing with Russian art."

Jake frowned. "That's not helpful."

Her smile widened. "Actually, it is. The real shipments of art go right to a small gallery downtown. The other shipments, which come much more regularly, land in a warehouse on Quai-Bickerdike. He also never exports from the gallery, but he does have shipments picked up from the warehouse. And those usually go across the border to the States."

"Hmmm. Anything else?"

"The pricing rarely changes for anything going to or from that warehouse. No matter how many items he's listed."

"So far, nothing illegal."

"True," she said. "But, he also buys bulk food and water the day before a shipment across the border. I think he's shipping something live."

Jake's eyes narrowed. "Human trafficking?"

She nodded.

His lips compressed as he surveyed what she'd found. "It's not enough for the police."

Her shoulders slumped.

"But it's enough for me," he said. "Let's go check out that warehouse."

She clenched her fist. "Yes." She stood up and winced when her weight landed on her left foot. Blood spotted the floor all around it.

Jake saw her foot and sighed. "Why would you sit here for two hours while your foot was bleeding?"

She shrugged. "I'll take care of it when I get home."

He stood up. "Sit back down. I'll be right back." He left the room with quick strides.

She stared after him for a moment. What was he doing? She shrugged and closed Mike's laptop. She should probably drop it off to him before she left. She snagged her heels from under the table. Blood soaked the inside of the left one. She was pretty sure they were ruined. And secretly she was glad. She never wanted to wear a pair of heels again.

She'd only taken one wincing step toward the door when Jake opened it again, holding a first-aid kit. He scowled. "I told you to sit and wait."

She scowled right back at him, standing her ground.

"I'm fine."

He walked over to her and stood inches away. "You're bleeding all over the floor."

Dani was tall for a woman at five-foot-eight, and Jake only stood at six feet, but his powerful build made her feel small and vulnerable. She didn't like it. She lifted her chin and reluctantly moved back to her chair.

She held out her hands for the first-aid kit, but he ignored her and knelt at her feet. She could tell his leg bothered him, since he didn't move with his usual grace.

"How's your leg?" she asked.

"Fine," he said tersely, as he lifted her bloody foot.

She shifted her weight and held the arms of the chair, forcing herself to be still.

"You don't like talking about it, do you?" she asked.

He shrugged. "Not much to say."

She raised her eyebrows and waited.

He sighed. "It aches, but that's nothing new. I'm fine."

The tough warrior who knelt at her feet did not like admitting any weakness, she thought. She could understand that and let the matter drop.

He inspected her foot. "You did a number on this one," he said. "I think there's something in there." He rummaged through the kit and pulled out a pair of tweezers. He held her ankle in a gentle but firm grip, and eased something out of the sole of her foot.

"A piece of glass. It's not big enough to need a stitch, but just big enough to be a problem if not looked after properly."

He took out antiseptic and bandages, and proceeded to doctor her foot.

She almost protested, but knew it would be useless. Instead she leaned back and let someone else take care of her. It was a strange feeling to have someone looking after her, even for something so minor.

"Why are you doing this?" she asked.

"Because feet can be awkward to do yourself." He looked up and studied her face. "Mostly because you were my partner tonight. You stay with your partner till the end. No matter what." He started packing up the first-aid kit.

She hadn't encountered much of that kind of loyalty in her life. She was sure her parents had been loyal to her, but they'd died in a car accident when she was ten and her memories of them were fading.

Chuck and Tassia were her two mainstays in life. She knew they were loyal to her, but she couldn't imagine either doing something like this.

"Is that what they taught you in SEAL training?"

He paused. "How'd you know I was a SEAL?"

"Hacker girl, remember?" She smiled. "I only snooped when Mike told me to crack into E.D.G.E. Don't worry, I didn't read your file."

Not all of it, she thought.

He nodded. "BUD/s is the first SEAL training course and one of the toughest things I've ever done. Rhys was my swim buddy. The first lesson drilled into us is you never, ever leave your swim buddy. You eat, do PT, and even go to the head with your swim buddy. You never leave them behind."

He shrugged. "It's ingrained in me." He stood up and rubbed a hand over the stubble on his chin. "I'm beat. Let's get out of here."

She stood up, pleased to find her foot ached a lot less with the glass out of it. It still throbbed, but it was manageable pain as far as she was concerned. She followed Jake into the hall and back to her office, where she grabbed her serviceable coat. She eased her feet into her black biker boots and zipped them up. So much more comfortable than those devil heels.

Jake watched her. "Nice look."

"What can I say? I'm a fashionista at heart."

He laughed. "Let's go. I'll walk you to your car."

She walked past him to the elevator and punched the button. "Don't worry about it, I'm fine."

She could feel him watching her back but she didn't turn to look at him.

He exhaled deeply. "Dani," he said. "How are you getting home?"

She pressed her lips together and turned around. "Usually I take the bus, okay? But I don't live far. Seriously, I'm good."

He rubbed his face again. "I've got a rental. I'll drive you." He held up his hand. "I'm too tired to argue. Let's go."

CHAPTER 11

"So what does a fighter and genius hacker do in her spare time?" Jake asked as he pulled out of the parking lot.

"Game and read."

Jake looked over at her. "Gaming I can see, but reading? I figured you'd be jumping out of planes or something else high adrenaline."

Dani laughed without meaning to. "No. I'm pretty boring. I love books."

He asked about her favorite books and told her his. Soon they were arguing over whether e-readers were better than paper.

It was close to four in the morning by the time Jake pulled into a spot in front of her building and put the car in park. Awkwardness descended like a smothering blanket. She unsnapped her seatbelt and grabbed her door handle. "Thanks for—"

His hand on her arm froze her. "Wait."

She paused but didn't face him.

"I wanted to apologize about the kiss earlier."

Dani closed her eyes briefly before sitting back and facing him. She forced a nonchalant expression on her face. "Don't bother. I know it was just for cover."

Jake nodded. "But I still want to apologize for it. I couldn't think of anything else to do when I saw that guard."

Dani shrugged and kept her tone even. "Well, at least Rhys wasn't your partner tonight."

His lips twitched. "So we're okay?"

She could see his relief that she wasn't going to make a big deal about the kiss. Did he think she wanted to be his girlfriend? Or that she'd start proclaiming her love? It was one kiss. Yes, a hot one, but still just a kiss.

"Sure. Just don't do it again," she said.

He frowned. "That doesn't sound like we're okay."

She rolled her eyes and lied smoothly. "Please. I've forgotten all about it. It's not like it was that great."

His jaw set. "You were the one who moaned."

She couldn't believe he'd brought that up. She shoved the car door open. "Yes. I'm a good actress." She swung her legs out and stood up, thankful to be out in the open.

"Wait." He leaned over the passenger seat. "Look, I don't want to fight. I just wanted to clear the air. The kiss? It won't happen again. I just wanted to say…for someone who hasn't done undercover work before, you did really well. And that's a compliment of the highest order." He smiled. "I'd work with you again, hacker girl."

The compliment didn't soothe her. "But only if you had to, right?" She shook her head. "Goodnight, Jake."

He muttered something before rattling off some numbers. "That's my cell. Call me tomorrow. I'll drive you to work."

She arched a brow. "We're not partners anymore, Jake. There's no need to coddle me."

He said the numbers again. "Just in case. Remember them."

"Fine. But I won't be calling. I can look after myself." She shut the door in his face.

Her exit was ruined when she stepped on her hurt foot and winced at the sudden rush of pain. She'd forgotten about it. She pushed it aside and hobbled to the front door, digging her key out. By the time she'd unlocked it, the car shut off behind her and Jake's door opened.

She huffed a breath. "I do not need your help, Jake. I'm—"

Strong arms lifted her into the air, literally sweeping her off her feet and cutting off her words.

"I know you can do this yourself," he said. "But I've had a long day and I want to make sure you get to your apartment okay." His scowl said he wanted to be doing anything but looking after her. She opened her mouth to protest and he cut her off. "Your friend was kidnapped by a powerful mafia family. I'm going to see you get upstairs and make sure your place is secure. Then I'll leave and you won't have to deal with me again."

She snapped her mouth shut, not knowing what to say as he carried her to the elevator and to her apartment on the fourth floor. At the door he set her gently on her feet. When she opened it, he held her back and stalked inside, his weapon in his hand.

She hobbled in, not seeing anyone. He came out of the bathroom and scowled at her. "You were supposed to wait in the hall."

Dani just waved him onward as she made her way to the couch, collapsing on it while Jake checked out the kitchen and her room. Exhaustion dragged at her and her eyes closed.

Something was tapping her cheek.

"Wake up, Dani."

Jake's deep voice. She cracked her eyelids. He crouched in front of her. She lay sideways on the couch in the fetal position, a blanket over her. His smile deepened.

"Don't you ever get tired?" she asked. It didn't seem fair that she could barely hold her eyes open and he looked as if he'd had eight hours of sleep.

"I'm tired," he said. "I'm just used to dealing with it." He paused and studied her for a moment. "Do you mind if

I ask you a question?"

"Do I need coffee for it?"

He shook his head. "I'm just wondering about your family. You haven't mentioned them, but we need to know if there's anyone else connected to you that the Rusakov family can find."

"No family. My parents died when I was ten," she said shortly. "Besides, I doubt Dmitri remembers me."

"And what about Vladimir?"

She stiffened and pulled the blanket more firmly around her. "He didn't see me tonight."

Jake tilted his head. "You're scared of him."

She scowled. "Well, I'm not stupid."

He shook his head slowly, his eyes never leaving her face. "No. It's more than that."

"I'm tired. You should go."

He moved to sit beside her on the couch. "How did you become a hacker?"

She blew out a breath. "If I tell you, will you leave?"

"If you want me to."

Oh, she wanted him to, and yet his presence comforted her. Her shoulders slumped. What harm would it be to answer a few questions? Chuck was always telling her she should open up to people.

"Computers were my escape," she said. "My foster families never really wanted me, just the extra cash they got for taking me in."

He nodded. "How did you meet the Rusakovs?"

"A friend." She scowled. "I *thought* he was a friend. Turns out the Rusakovs wanted more hackers working for them. They paid him to troll for some. He found me."

"I'm sorry," Jake said. "So Dmitri approached you?"

She yawned and shook her head. "His son, Vladimir. The charmer."

Jake stilled. "He charmed you?"

She hugged herself. "Is this really necessary? I was fourteen and Vladimir was nineteen. I had a crush and he used it to get what he wanted. I was stupid, okay?"

Jake rested a hand on her knee and squeezed. "You weren't stupid," he said. "You were young and alone."

She bit her lip and stared at her hands. "Is the inquisition over?"

"When did you find the courage to leave?" he asked.

So it wasn't over. She blamed being tired for the reason she didn't fight answering his questions. In a way it felt good to answer, as if something inside was cracking open and letting in fresh air. She could breathe just a bit easier.

"The first time, I didn't leave—I got sent to juvie. Spent six months there. It sucked. By the end, I was determined to turn over a new leaf." She swallowed.

Jake took her cold hand in one of his and rubbed his calloused thumb over her palm. Back and forth, over and over.

She took a shuddering breath. "Vladimir found me after I got out and said the Rusakovs owned me. I could either work as a hacker or a whore." She shrugged. "I had no one to turn to. So I chose computers. Not long after, Vladimir decided I should be one of his girlfriends."

Jake's thumb stilled.

She might as well tell him everything. "I *dated* Vladimir for two years. I hated every minute of it. I told myself at least I wasn't a whore." She pressed her lips together. "But I was just lying to myself."

Jake continued to rub her palm and she stared at it, not seeing their hands, but the nightmare of that time.

"I started taking on more and more dangerous jobs for the Rusakovs. I think…I think I *wanted* to be caught."

She lifted her head. "One night, I broke into a financial company to get into their servers. I could have done it from a secure computer elsewhere, but I wanted, no *needed,* the thrill of breaking into the building." She shrugged. "I tripped an alarm." She smiled. "Chuck was the detective in charge of my case."

"What happened next?"

"I asked him to help me get out of the life." She remembered sitting in front of him, her hands gripped so tight her knuckles looked like white bone. But his eyes had reminded her of her father's. So she'd gathered her courage and asked for help.

"So he did?"

"I gave him information on the Rusakovs and he helped me fake my death," she said.

Jake's thumb stopped for a moment before stroking again. She couldn't bring herself to look at him. "Vladimir liked to fight and show how tough he was. Usually, I kept out of the way, but one day I stepped in front of his knife."

His hand squeezed hers now. "You could have died."

"It was worth the risk." She finally raised her head. "I owe Chuck my life. I checked into the hospital under D. Everett, an alias I'd already created. Chuck and his partner were the ones who went to Vladimir's door to tell him Danika Kashnikov was dead."

"Danika. I like it." Then he frowned. "That worked?"

Dani smiled. "Chuck can be very convincing. He also implied my death looked suspicious. Vladimir was happy to state that he didn't know me, and then proceeded to take a very long vacation in Russia. After that it was just a matter of settling into my new identity."

"Why didn't you leave Montreal?"

"Money," she said with a shrug. "I've been saving ever since, but it takes quite a bit to start over in a new city. And I didn't think Vladimir would come back." She shook her head. "Stupid of me."

"You're not stupid." Jake still hadn't let go of her hand. "Are you still planning on leaving?"

She stared at the floor. His fingers touched her chin and turned her face to his. "Dani?"

"This is my home," she whispered. "I don't want to leave."

His eyes turned to granite. "Then we're going to nail this bastard so you don't have to."

Something lightened inside her. She believed him, she realized. And when he leaned toward her, she met him halfway.

His soft lips pressed against hers, and her fatigue vanished, replaced by a tingling awareness of Jake's nearness. All her senses focused on him and his strength. He smelled of soap and man. His calloused hand stroked her jawline before digging into her hair.

He pulled back and a small groan escaped her. When she dragged her eyes open, he smiled and brushed her hair back from her face with both hands. He cupped her head and gave her a short, hard kiss, before jumping up from the couch. "I should leave now," he said, his voice gruff.

She didn't want him to, but she found the words to ask him to stay stuck in her throat. She bit her lip and his eyes tracked the movement. "If you want," she whispered.

"What I want," he said in almost a growl, "is to take you to your bedroom, strip you naked, and then do all sorts of delicious things to your body."

She sucked in a breath, her brain frozen, her body alive and wanting.

"But I can't," he said. He ran a hand through his hair. "We work together. And you're vulnerable right now. It's not right." He swallowed and went to her door. "Lock up behind me."

Dani rolled over in bed to stare at her clock. Five in the morning. The gray light of predawn illuminated her bedroom, so she could see her twisted sheets and the pillow she'd thrown across the room.

Damn Jake.

He'd left her emotions whirling and her body humming. Like a drug high, she knew this attraction she felt for Jake would blow through her like a hurricane, leaving her wrecked and exhausted. It was definitely something she should leave alone.

She pressed her lips together. She wasn't going to sleep anytime soon; she might as well get up and see what else she could find out about the Rusakov properties. She pulled an oversized hoodie on over her tank and sleep shorts and padded out to the kitchen in her bare feet.

She'd only just started her coffeepot when a knock sounded on the door. Was it Jake? Her heart began to race. No matter that she'd just decided to stay away from him, she went to the door to check the peephole.

As she got to the door it burst open, hitting her arm and face, stunning her for an instant. Three men leapt into the room, shutting the door behind them. Two grabbed her arms, holding them tight behind her back. The Gromov brothers.

The third man smiled at her, his face craggy and pitted, while he pulled his Glock from a holster under his jacket.

Adrenaline shot like lightning from her center out to her limbs. Her hands clenched into fists, preparing to fight. The men behind her tightened their grips. She'd have bruises on her upper arms tomorrow.

"Peace, Danika." The heavy Russian accent made a harsh

k sound in her name. Dani-*ka*. She shivered at the sound of it and the memories it stirred. The man held his Glock in a light grip. His hair was dark, short and receding, giving an impression of an overly large forehead above his dark eyes. He had a small bump on his nose, a remnant from the time she'd broken it. He rubbed it now.

"Petroff," Dani said with a nod. "What are you doing here?"

"Did you really think Vladimir wouldn't recognize you? He saw you in the crowd." He shook his head. "We've known for a while that you were alive. But for old time's sake, Dmitri let you live, as long as you stayed away from Vlad. But you've gone too far, Danika." Petroff nodded at one of the man behind her. "You really should have stayed dead."

The sharp prick of a needle entered her neck. She struggled and they laughed before releasing her.

Panic burned her. Her vision blurred and she staggered to the kitchen, pulling a knife from the block on the counter. Panting, she faced Petroff, who'd followed her. Her knees buckled and darkness seared the edges of her sight.

"Wha…did you do?" She grabbed the counter as she slid down, but her fingers weren't working. She couldn't feel them. The knife clattered to the floor. Her body no longer responded, no matter what she wanted it to do. She fell sideways and knew no more.

Jake parked his rental and got out. He stood in front of Dani's place. It was only just past noon. He knew she hadn't had much sleep, but he'd been surprised when she hadn't shown up this morning. She'd seemed eager to look into the warehouse with him. He'd held off going to see if she'd come in late, but he didn't want to wait any longer.

She hadn't picked up her phone earlier, so he'd decided drastic measures were needed. He grabbed the lattes from inside his car and went to wake her up.

A nice neighbor let him trail her through the lobby door. He took the elevator to the right floor and refused to think about why he was so eager to see Dani. He wondered if she was feisty in the morning, or if sleep made her more pliable.

He grinned as he rapped sharply on her door. No answer. He knocked again. When there was still no answer, he pulled out his cell and punched in her number.

He could hear it ringing inside the apartment. Strange. He hadn't pegged her for such a heavy sleeper. He twisted the handle automatically and stiffened when it turned easily in his hand.

Her door was unlocked.

He set the coffees down and eased the door open, listening. He waited a full minute before entering and when he did, he went in low and fast, his Sig in hand.

It took only seconds for him to clear the apartment. She wasn't there, but the black clutch she'd used yesterday sat open on the hall table with her phone and wallet in it. The bloodstained heels lay on the floor below. Something about seeing those heels made his gut clench.

He walked the apartment again, noting the neatness in the living room, the sparseness of Dani's bedroom—almost as if she was afraid of having possessions. He stopped in the kitchen.

A butcher knife lay on the floor.

It felt like metal bands constricted his chest as his heart rate accelerated. He forced himself to breath deeply and hold it for two counts before exhaling.

He pulled out his cell and punched some numbers. "Blackwell? We've got a problem."

"How much did you give her?" The deep voice growled near Dani. It made her want to curl in on herself, easing back into the dark.

Pain lanced her cheek, shocking her into stillness. Something small inside her began gibbering in panic, telling her to scream, to run. That *he* had her.

No. She dove back into the darkness, refusing to open her eyes. It was much nicer here. No pain. No hurt.

"Wake up!" Something struck her head, whipping it backward. She kept her body loose and her breathing heavy as awareness trickled in.

She'd been drugged. Her limbs felt weighted down and numb, and a great darkness waited for her. But she didn't let herself fall just yet.

Something warm and rough touched her cheek. A hand. It cradled her head. "Come on, Danika." The voice was still deep, but gentle, concerned. "Wake for me, darling. I need to ask you a question."

She almost opened her eyes to see him.

"Danika, you little bitch," the voice crooned. "Open your eyes, or I'm going to pluck them out."

Fear froze her insides. Vladimir.

Breathe, she thought. Breathe heavy. The darkness receded further, pushed away by the adrenaline spiking through her.

She couldn't hear anything besides a low conversation in Russian, too far away for her to make out. She didn't dare open her eyes. Her skin prickled with cold. Her hoodie was open and she lay on a bare concrete floor.

"Petroff," the voice growled above her. "When will she wake? We need to know who sent her to the party."

Her heart skipped as his hand wrapped around her neck.

"Why don't I just kill her?" Petroff grumbled.

"We need to find out what she knows," Vladimir repeated. His hand tightened on her neck and she forced herself to stillness.

"Her heart rate is picking up," he said.

Dani steeled herself for what was coming. She'd seen Vladimir do this too many times before.

He grabbed her breast through her tank top, pinching and twisting it hard. Her stomach clenched in response, but she did nothing else. Fear enabled her to stay separate from the pain. Her life depended on it.

"Hmmm," he said. He let go of her breast. "Well, it shouldn't be long now. Throw her in a cage. I'll deal with her when she's coherent."

Dani felt herself being lifted and then dropped onto the floor again. A clang of metal and then the click of a lock.

The darkness inside her rushed up and she met it willingly.

CHAPTER 12

Jake paced the control room at E.D.G.E. "Where would they take her?"

"Are you sure they've got her?" Koven asked from a desk nearby. He had his laptop open, but was watching Jake instead.

"She wouldn't just disappear," Jake growled.

Koven shrugged. "Not true, according to her file. She might have decided it was too hot to stay. She's good at disappearing."

The thought had crossed Jake's mind, but he trusted his instincts. He shook his head. "No, they've taken her. The question is, when and where."

"If they've got her, then she's at Rusakov's mansion. That's where they typically carry out most of their business.

Besides, if Dmitri wanted to see her, you can bet that he wouldn't go to *her*."

Jake paced again. They'd had two operators staking out the mansion since the party the night before. "What about that warehouse Dani found in the files?"

"It's down on Quai-Bickerdick. Way too public for this kind of business." Koven held up a hand when Jake went to protest. "I've sent one of my agents there to check it out. He's got eyes on and there's no movement. As soon as he sees something, he'll report in."

"She could have been missing for hours. We need men looking for her."

Koven compressed his lips. "I agree, but we can't just charge into a family home. We wait for the warrant."

Jake growled and Koven raised his hand. "I get how you feel. Don't worry, the judge I called owes me a favor."

His cell rang. "Yes?" Koven listened for a few moments and then shut it off. He closed his laptop and stood. "The warrant's in. We can send an assault team to the mansion." He moved toward the weapons room. "You coming?"

Jake's gut clenched. It didn't feel right. His instincts had saved his life more than once on missions. And right now, they were screaming at him to go to the warehouse.

He shook his head. There were enough operators going to the mansion that he didn't need to be there.

Rhys strode down the hallway toward them. "I just heard they took hacker girl. Let's rock and roll, College."

"Wait out. Let the others take this."

"You sure?" Koven asked, scrutinizing him.

Jake nodded, ignoring Rhys's quizzical look. "Rhys and I will go back up your operator at the warehouse."

Koven paused for a moment. "You'll need a team, then. Let me send Cat and Zach with you."

"Can they handle themselves?"

Koven shrugged. "They're E.D.G.E. operators, just back from a mission." He said it as if that was guarantee enough. "Let me know if you have any luck with the warehouse."

Jake hoped for Dani's sake that he wouldn't need luck.

Someone had glued her eyelids together. She turned her head and groaned as lightning shot through it. She rubbed at her eyes and forced them open, feeling as if she'd been in a sandstorm and just didn't remember.

How long had she been out? She shivered as she tried to remember what had happened. She lay in her skimpy pajamas and hoodie on a cold cement floor. Rolling to her side, she swallowed hard as nausea welled in her. Thick metal bars stood next to her face. She squinted as she scanned her surroundings.

The room was concrete, gray, gray, and more gray, broken only by the metal cages lining the walls, one of which held her. A padlock secured the door.

Her heart started to pound and her head decided to play in time with it. Her breast throbbed where Vladimir had twisted it, but the nausea receded and her head cleared, leaving her cold and more than a little scared.

"Come on, Dani," she whispered to herself. "Don't give up now."

Distant sounds of traffic and even a boat's horn drifted to her. From what she could see, the room beyond was large and bare, with flecks of something dark smearing the floor and wall inside another cage across from her. A square patch of sunshine glowed on the floor in front of her.

She gripped the steel bars and dragged herself to standing. A woman lay in one of the far cages near the window, her blonde hair covering her face, her dress torn and grimy.

Adrenaline flooded her system.

"Tass?" she called. "Tassia, is that you?"

The figure didn't move. Dani shook the door of her cage. Had they drugged her? She couldn't even see if the woman was breathing. She had to get out of here.

She slid her hands through the bars to look at the lock on the door. Standard padlock. Her breathing evened out. This, she could deal with. She'd been too tired last night to take her hair out of the chignon it had been in. It was still piled on top of her head, albeit much messier now. She pushed her fingers through it, searching. She pulled out her special lock-pick hairpins.

Within seconds she had the padlock undone.

Let's hear it for bedhead, she thought as she shoved the pins back into her hair.

She ran to the cage where the woman lay. "Tassia?"

No response. Dani reached through the bars and grabbed the woman's shoulder. She rolled limply onto her back, her sightless eyes staring at the ceiling.

Dani snatched her hand back. It wasn't Tassia, but the woman—or rather, girl, from the looks of her—had bruises mottling her face and neck.

Dani swallowed. Not Tassia, but someone who'd gotten on the Rusakovs' bad side. She clenched her fists. She needed to find Tass soon.

The window in the back of the room was narrow and high. She had to jump to look out. She could make out the top of another brick building nearby, but that was it.

In the last cage, opposite the dead girl, was a pair of strappy black-and-silver heels with vibrant red soles. She stilled, knowing where she'd last seen those shoes.

She reached through the bars for them, her hand trembling slightly. Size 9. Tassia's.

These were her favorite heels. She wore them on special occasions and first dates. Apparently, the red sole meant they were something special. Dani hugged the shoes to her chest.

Tass had been here. She sucked in a breath. Maybe she was still here. She turned to the door.

Time to find Tass and get the hell out.

Dani breathed a sigh of relief when she found the door unlocked. It opened onto a narrow hallway that ran in both directions. She couldn't hear traffic anymore; instead, the muffled sounds of machinery or engines of some sort echoed through the building. She turned right and passed two other closed doors, both locked.

The hall ended in a T-junction. On one side was an emergency exit. She leapt toward it. The small viewing window showed a rusty fire escape, and more warehouses beyond this one. She was about three stories up. A large sign on the door said an alarm would sound if opened.

Dani hesitated. This was her chance to escape. She could lose any pursuers without problems. The other end of the hall had a similar door with a large glass window, but this one looked out over the interior of the warehouse.

If she left now, she'd lose her chance to look for Tass. Her friend was counting on her. She stepped away from the exit, deciding to check the other rooms quickly and then leave.

She ran to the other door and peeked out the window. It led to a metal walkway that encircled the upper level of the warehouse proper and overlooked the floor, as well as a set of stairs leading down. Shipping crates lined one wall, floor to ceiling.

A large truck was parked near the warehouse's garage-style doors at the far end. Men with automatic rifles herded a group of about twenty women into the back of the truck. The women huddled together, keeping as far from the guns as they could.

They were going to deliver the next shipment.

She needed to call Jake and the others. They had to stop this. She took a few more seconds, straining her eyes, but she couldn't see Tass among the women. That didn't mean she still wasn't here somewhere, locked in one of the rooms.

Dani needed help. But first she needed a phone. The first room near her was unlocked. Filing cabinets, their drawers half open and empty, stood side-by-side with a scratched-up desk, its drawers also open. On the desk beside a metal lamp were a phone and some scattered papers.

A large window overlooked the warehouse below. She kept out of sight as she snatched up the telephone. She debated for half a second before dialing E.D.G.E.'s main number. It was the only number from the office that she knew by heart. She promised herself that in the future she'd memorize all her important numbers instead of relying on her cell.

"Hello, E.D.G.E. Securities. We go to the Edge so you don't have to. How may I help you?"

Merde. What was Ashley doing answering the phone? She must be covering for the main receptionist. Her smooth voice sounded professional and courteous. Dani knew that would change soon enough.

"Ashley, I need to speak with Mr. Blackwell." She stared out the window. The women had been loaded and Vladimir's men shut the truck's door. The door to the warehouse rose while two of the men got into the front of the truck.

"Danielle?" Ashley said. "Is that you? Why do you want to speak to Blackwell?"

"Ashley, I don't have much time. Please, put me through."

There was a chilly pause. "I'm afraid I can't just put anyone through to Mr. Blackwell. Why don't you give me a message and I'll pass it up."

Dani set her jaw. "Fine. I'm trapped in a warehouse with the Russian mob. I need backup."

Another pause. Then a delicate snort sounded in her ear. "Goodbye, Danielle."

The dial tone sounded. "Shit." She paused only a moment and then dialed another number, praying she remembered it correctly.

"Harrison."

His gruff voice made her shoulders loosen slightly. "Jake? I need help."

"Dani, where are you?"

A coaster lying among the papers on the desk caught her eye. "Some warehouse," she said. "I heard a boat horn earlier. I'm guessing it's the same warehouse I found in the files last night."

Jake cursed and said something to someone else. She picked up the coaster and shoved it into her hoodie pocket to look at later, before rifling through the papers. Nothing important.

Jake came back online. "Rhys and I are almost there. There's an operator outside. Can you get out?"

She thought of the emergency door, but dismissed it. She needed to find Tass. "Don't worry about me. There's a bunch of women on a truck that's just leaving. I can't see the license plate." She looked out the window again. Her heart stopped and she swore under her breath.

"Dani?" Jake's voice was even. "What's going on?"

Vladimir and Petroff were coming up the stairs. Vladimir held a phone to his ear, while Petroff carried a jerrycan.

"I've got to go," she said.

"Wait. Where are you?"

She couldn't wait any longer. "Office. Top floor." She hung up the phone and dove under the desk. The door to the office opened seconds later and she held her breath as footsteps drew closer to the desk.

Vladimir spoke in Russian. "Are you sure? We don't even know what the bitch was doing there."

The desk creaked when he leaned against it. "Yes, Father. But if you give me time, I can get everything out of her. You know we have history together."

Dani's heart pounded in her chest. He was talking about her. She knew what Vladimir was capable of. She shivered and concentrated on breathing silently.

"Yes. We'll torch it all. Nothing will connect back to us." A small pause. "Don't worry, Father. I'll take care of her." A click, then Vladimir swore. "Petroff, bring her to me."

"You got it." The door opened and shut.

Vladimir moved to the door and was quiet for a moment. She concentrated on not breathing hard. Liquid hit the floor, making splashing sounds. A lot of liquid. She swallowed a gasp as the acrid scent of gasoline overwhelmed her.

The office door opened again and a lighter scratched. Her

chest seized at the whoosh of fire catching and swooping through the room.

CHAPTER 13

J ake cursed again and put his cell away. "Koven's agent isn't picking up."

Rhys steered their rental smoothly through traffic on the AutoRoute Bonaventure getting to the dock they needed. "I haven't seen you this worked up in a while, College. You need to relax. We'll get there."

Jake's muscles tightened and he wanted to punch something. He couldn't relax. And that was the whole problem. He was too invested in this. Too invested in Dani. He needed calm to work, but he wasn't sure he was going to find it in time.

"Just get us there, Lucky," he said.

The car accelerated. "Roger that."

Jake checked the side mirror and saw the other E.D.G.E.

car carrying their backup: Cat, a blonde Amazon of a woman who'd led the team that had rescued them in Afghanistan, and Zach, a fierce dark-skinned man who was her second-in-command.

Zach had also been on their rescue mission, Jake remembered. They seemed competent enough, but he hadn't worked or trained with them. He didn't know how they'd respond in a firefight, and not knowing just added to his tension.

A few minutes later, Rhys screeched to a halt less than a block from the designated warehouse. Jake jumped out and found the dark sedan parked on the corner. Had to be the CSIS agent's car. He jogged over to it, keeping watch on the building.

A small hole in the driver's window warned him before he got too close. No wonder the agent hadn't answered the calls. Jake looked through the glass and saw a brown-haired man slumped over onto the passenger's seat. The exit wound from the bullet had literally blown the man's brains all over the interior of the car.

Rhys joined him, studying the dead man. "Was he E.D.G.E.?"

"No. Koven needed more men to watch all the Rusakov properties, so he called CSIS."

Both men strode back to their vehicle and out of direct sight of the warehouse. Cat and Zach waited for them, weapons out and discreetly by their sides.

"They know we're watching," Rhys said.

"Worse," Jake said, looking back at the building. "They're expecting us." He pulled his Sig Sauer from his back holster. "Koven wanted us to call it in and wait for a team if there was anything to report."

Rhys grinned. "Good thing he's not our boss."

Cat narrowed her eyes at Rhys before asking Jake, "How do you want to play this?"

"Hard and fast. Weapons free," Jake said.

Cat arched a brow. "Weapons free? This isn't Afghanistan. We can't just shoot anyone we want."

He jerked his head back toward the dead agent's car. "It's confirmed enemy territory. Weapons free, soldier."

"Copy that," Cat said. Zach nodded and both flicked their safeties off.

Jake watched both Cat and Zach for a moment, needing to know that they'd be with him totally. "This is a rescue op. Dani's on the top floor, some kind of office." His muscles tensed at the thought. "Now, let's go see if there's a back door to this place."

Dani pulled part of her hoodie up over her mouth while she breathed. Smoke had filled the room incredibly fast and the heat smothered her. She began to cough and knew she didn't have long before the smoke overwhelmed her.

No longer worried about Vladimir, she crawled out from under the desk and made her way to the door, avoiding the blaze crawling up the walls as much as possible. Thankfully, he must have poured the gasoline around the edges of the room, so she still had a narrow path to the door. Her eyes watered, blurring her vision even more. She peeked out the window but couldn't see Vladimir, so she slipped out of the office, coughing from the smoke she'd inhaled. A few deep breaths later and she felt the muscles in her chest easing.

Tassia obviously wasn't in the building if they planned to burn it down. Time for her to leave. She turned to the fire exit at the end of the hall.

Petroff strode around the corner, blocking her exit.

She bolted through the near door leading to the metal walkway, and ran into a solid chest. Hands grabbed her arms and held her tight.

"*Kotyonok*," Vladimir's smooth voice said, calling her by the hated nickname. "Just the woman I was looking for."

"Get your hands off me, asshole." She brought her knee up, but he twisted at the last moment, avoiding it.

"Petroff, take her." Vladimir shoved her and she stumbled back. An arm came around her neck and she only barely had time to tuck her chin and slip a hand between her neck and his arm, trying to stop him from cutting off her air.

"Do you want to question her?" Petroff asked.

"No. Father wants her taken care of. He doesn't want me involved with her again." Vladimir looked at her and shook his head. "It's too bad, *Kotyonok*. We could have used your skills again. You shouldn't have gone against Dmitri."

"I didn't," she croaked, still trying to separate Petroff's

beefy arm from her neck. Maybe she could lie her way out. "It was just a party. I just…just wanted to see you."

His eyes narrowed, then he shook his head. "I don't believe you, Danika. Father might, but I know you better. You don't do anything without planning."

She tried to shake her head, trying to think of anything to stall them. "Okay. Fine," she said. "But I'm only looking for my friend. She went missing after she dated you."

Vladimir's face cleared. "Tassia." He said her name in the voice he used for seduction, like dark velvet rubbing over bare skin. "She had more fight in her than I expected. She almost reminded me of you." He stepped closer and trailed a finger down the side of her face not being squeezed by the Neanderthal behind her. She would have puked if she could.

"What did you do with her?" she demanded.

"Not too much. Though I did give her to Petroff to play with, didn't I?" Vladimir grinned.

Dani kicked out at him, but Petroff squeezed his arm tighter around her neck and jerked her away. She choked. "Where is she?"

Vladimir shrugged. "That's not what you should be worried about. Goodbye, *Kotyonok*." He looked at Petroff. "Take care of her. But do it somewhere else. And get rid of the body in the cage. We don't need bones found by the fire department."

Vladimir turned and jogged down the metal stairs to the main floor.

"Come on," Petroff said, pushing her toward the stairs.

She couldn't let him take her anywhere. Reaching back with her free hand, she found his face. He squeezed her neck harder, cutting off her meager supply of air. She scratched at his cheek as her lungs burned and her head pounded. Darkness blurred her vision when she finally found his eye and used her thumb to dig in.

"Fuck," he shouted and flung her away from him.

Unable to stop herself, she fell to the walkway, rolling to the edge. She gasped in a single breath before the feeling of openness behind her sent adrenaline rushing from her core and down her limbs.

She lunged for any kind of hold in that split second before she fell. Her hands grabbed the edge and gripped tight as she toppled over the side.

The weight of her body pulled on her shoulders and a scream ripped from her throat as she dangled three stories above the concrete floor.

"Stupid bitch," Petroff said. He pulled a gun from under the back of his shirt.

He raised it and she stared down the barrel, debating whether to let go, wondering if she'd survive the fall. She certainly wouldn't survive a bullet through the head.

A smirk crawled over Petroff's face. "I never liked you. I could never see what Vladimir saw in you."

She adjusted her grip. "Jealous, were you?"

His face reddened. "I'm gonna enjoy this." He bent closer.

The crack of a gunshot sounded and he jerked back with a grunt of pain.

"Dani," Jake shouted.

She looked down. Jake stood there, in a classic firing stance, his gun trained on Petroff. Rhys stood at his back, gun out and scanning the warehouse. She could see two other operators back near the crates. The truck with the women and the men guarding it were nowhere in sight.

Petroff lumbered up to the edge of the walkway, holding his bleeding shoulder and aiming his gun below.

"Watch out," she shouted.

Petroff's gun went off and sounded louder than she'd expected. A quick look showed Jake and Rhys taking cover behind the metal shipping crates. They returned fire. Petroff scuttled back to the hallway of offices, but even from her vantage point she could see the thick smoke through the window. He continued to fire his gun.

"Hang on, Dani," Jake shouted.

"Hang on?" she muttered. "Screw that." She'd had enough of pretending she was a trapeze artist. She swung her leg onto the walkway and pulled herself up onto her stomach. She lay there for a moment, breathing heavily.

Hot metal touched her cheek and she jerked away. Petroff stood over her with the barrel of his gun against her face. Now he pressed it against the back of her head. "Get up," he growled.

She slowly stood and raised her hands. He pulled her back against his body and put the gun to her temple.

"Down the stairs."

They moved slowly to the metal stairs. Jake and the others had stopped firing. Dani couldn't see or hear them anymore. She swallowed hard as Petroff forced her down the first steps.

Jake appeared on the landing below them. She knew his gun was trained on Petroff, but it looked as though he was pointing it straight at her.

"You okay, Dani?" he asked her, though he never took his eyes from Petroff.

"Yeah, I'm great. Except for the gun pointed at my head." She'd never been able to control her mouth in tense situations. She compressed her lips. Maybe she should start avoiding tense situations.

"Shut up," Petroff said, tightening his arm around her neck.

She coughed. "Easy, big guy."

"Out of the way," Petroff said to Jake. "Or I'm gonna blow your girl's brains all over this warehouse."

Jake stilled and kept complete focus on Petroff. "Do you trust me, Dani?"

What was she supposed to say to that? "Trust you with what, exactly? I really don't even know you that well." She grunted when Petroff's arm tightened further.

Jake's sigh was loud, but his gaze never left Petroff. "Just answer the question. Do you trust me?"

She really wished she could sigh, but she could barely breathe with Petroff slowly cutting off her air. Did she trust

Jake? Her body seemed to respond rather than her mind. "Yes."

"Then don't move."

Petroff moved them both down another step. He kept most of his bulk behind her body.

"I don't really have much choice about this," she said.

"She'll move if I tell her to move," Petroff said. "Now where's your friend? Get him where I can see him. I don't feel like getting shot in the back."

Jake nodded while still watching Petroff with that focused, predatory look. Rhys called out from below. He must have been watching closely. "I'm here," he said as he stepped from behind a crate. He too had a gun trained on her. Or rather, Petroff, she reminded herself.

She wondered if she should go limp in Petroff's arms so Jake could shoot him, or if that would just piss Petroff off. As her mind raced, Petroff forced them down another two steps. Closer and closer to the landing and Jake.

"Move," Petroff said. "Or I'll shoot your girlfriend."

Jake didn't move. "She's not my girlfriend. Like the lady said, she doesn't know me that well."

Petroff moved them down one more step. They now stood only about ten feet from Jake. Dani could see satisfaction in Jake's eyes. Her heart rate sped up. *Merde*. He was going to shoot. Didn't he know how dangerous that was?

"Don't do it," she said.

"What?" Jake asked, not looking at her.

"Don't shoot him. I'm pretty sure the brain can still send

impulses after it dies. He could still pull the trigger." She swallowed. "I'll still be dead."

She felt Petroff move her more securely in front of him.

Jake sighed again. "We're gonna have to work on that trust issue, Dani. Now remember what I said."

Not to move. Oh god. She almost waved her arms at him. She wanted to squeeze her eyes shut, but focused instead on Jake. He stood tall and strong before them, an immovable wall. Could he do it?

"You're not gonna shoot," Petroff said. "Now, get out of my way."

Jake didn't move. He didn't even look like he was breathing. "Not gonna happen. If you shoot her, you're dead. What's your next move? We gonna wait here till the cops show up?"

Petroff growled. "If you don't move I'll shoot her in the knee first."

"She'll live."

Dani almost protested, but something about Jake radiated danger at that moment, more so than Petroff. Don't move. *Trust him*, her inner voice told her. She bit her lip. She really didn't have much choice in the matter. But she also really didn't want to limp for the rest of her life.

"I'm not bluffing," Petroff said.

She felt more than saw the gun move away from her temple as Petroff lowered it to shoot her in the leg. A sound of protest escaped her lips, but her eyes stayed trained on Jake's gun.

Time slowed. She saw Jake's finger pull back on the trigger and light flashed from the muzzle. A concussion of sound hit her. Petroff's arm loosened and his body dropped. She stood paralyzed with shock for the first time in her life, her wide eyes on Jake.

He looked at her for the first time, moving toward her, lowering his gun. Her mouth opened but no words came out. Her mind was blank. Jake's mouth was moving. She focused on it, concentrating past the tinny whine that rang in her ears.

"Are you okay?" he asked, his hand holding her shoulder.

She nodded, automatically turning to Petroff, but Jake's hand stopped her. "Don't look," he advised. "It's…messy."

Being shot in the face will do that to a person.

Jake snorted and Dani realized she'd spoken out loud. She nodded, though no question had been asked. "Okay," she said. She moved past Jake to the next flight of stairs. "Okay. I'm okay."

Jake was right next to her and she moved a little bit away. "I'm okay," she said again.

"Yup," was all he said. But he stayed right beside her.

They reached the bottom. Blood started to pool on the concrete floor, dripping from the steps above. The little pools started to get bigger.

"Dani?" Jake's voice was gentle. "We have to go. The place is on fire."

"What?" She continued to stare at the blood.

A finger under her chin lifted her face. She looked into

Jake's concerned gaze. "Stay with me."

She straightened her shoulders and nodded. "Right. I'm here. I'm okay."

His lips twisted. "You're not okay." He dropped his hand. "But you will be."

Rhys strode up to them, his eyes constantly scanning the area. "Ready to move?"

Jake nodded. "Let's go."

Dani took a deep breath and lifted her eyes to see Petroff's body lying on the stairs above her. His arm dangled over the side.

"That's for what you did to Tass," she whispered.

CHAPTER 14

The debrief lasted until well after dinner. Dani huddled for warmth in her hoodie and borrowed sweatpants. Her stomach rumbled dangerously as everyone filed out of the conference room—or war room, as she was beginning to think of it. Chuck squeezed Dani's shoulder as he walked past. She was glad he didn't stay behind. She wasn't up for any more talking. The door shut after the last person left.

She let her head drop forward and closed her eyes. Fatigue and guilt weighed heavy on her.

The whisper of sound didn't surprise her. She'd known somehow that he'd stay. She didn't move when Jake sat in the chair beside her.

"You did good, you know," he said.

The words bounced off the armor of guilt she wore. "I failed." She lifted her head and stared at Jake. "Tassia is still missing."

Jake studied her a moment. "But because of you, we know for sure who has her and where she's probably headed."

"That is, if she's not already dead."

"They won't kill her."

Dani swallowed hard. "Yet. You mean they won't kill her yet."

"We have a bit of time. And now we have a lead." He pointed to the coaster that sat in the middle of the table. The coaster she'd snagged from the desk in the warehouse. "That's from a strip club in New York. You heard Blackwell. We've already got people checking it out."

She clenched her fists. "There's got to be more we can do."

Jake took her fists in his hands and opened them, massaging the tension out of them. "There is. You can get some rest and be ready for whatever they ask you to do next."

"But I'm not a field operator. I'm not even an IT tech anymore. I'm on probation until they can decide if I'm an *asset* to the team." She spat out the words.

Jake shrugged. "Everyone has to start somewhere. It means you have to prove you can work with a team. A partner." He tossed the words at her as if he expected them to explode. Or rather her.

She compressed her lips together. "I can do that. I've

already shown I can do that."

Jake slowly shook his head. "You don't trust anyone."

"I trusted you." The words were out before she could analyze them. She hadn't wanted to say them, but now that they were out she might as well follow through. "I trusted you when you shot Petroff."

Jake arched a brow. "You barely trusted me, even though I'm a Navy SEAL and I could have made that shot at fifty yards, let alone five."

She blew out a breath. "So what are you saying?"

"If you're going to be on my team, you've got to trust me. You've got to do what I say, when I say it." His intense gaze seared her and his hands squeezed hers. "Our lives could depend on it."

She wanted to turn away, but she couldn't escape his gaze. So she deflected with words. "Do you trust me?"

Something flickered in his eyes. "To a point."

She sat back. He didn't trust her. Somehow that fact mattered to her. She pulled her hands from his.

"Listen," he continued. "You're on probation. You're lucky they're letting you help. I'll be in charge, which means you can't question my calls."

She held up her hands to stop his speech, trying to process what was happening. "Wait. So it's okay for you not to trust me, but you're demanding my trust?"

He went to speak but she stopped him by standing up. "And I'm *lucky* they're letting me help?" She slammed a palm onto the table. "They're freaking lucky I helped them, or they wouldn't have the information they do. And you better believe I'm going to get my friend back with or without your help."

Jake watched Dani storm out of the room. How the hell was he going to work with her? She let her emotions control her. The anger sparking in her eyes stirred him.

He cursed silently. Who was he kidding? His emotions controlled him when she was around. Emotions didn't go well with missions. If he was smart, he'd back off this one. Though both Knight and Blackwell wanted him to take the lead on this, to get a taste of what being a field operator for E.D.G.E. meant.

He stood and followed Dani. She was in more danger than she realized, which was why he wanted her close. She strode in her borrowed clothes to the elevator. Did she really think she could just go home?

"Where are you going?" he asked her when he stood beside her.

Her eyes flared and color bloomed on her cheeks. Feisty thing. He asked her the question again just to see the angry sparks in her eyes.

"Home. I need to grab clothes and my wallet."

"I can't let you do that," he said, and almost laughed at her outraged gasp, but she'd had a hard day so he stopped needling her. "You can't go home," he said. "Your apartment is compromised. They could be waiting for you."

"Dammit." She sighed. "I just want my stuff."

"Look, I'll have Rhys swing by first to check it out. If it's clear, then we'll give you two minutes to grab what you need."

The elevator dinged open. Some blonde woman stood there holding files, her high sleek ponytail swinging as she perused Dani from head to toe.

"Really, Danielle? You look like you slept in an alley after a date gone wrong," she drawled. "I don't really think the higher-ups at E.D.G.E. would approve."

Dani flushed and Jake's anger surged when she just looked away and stepped onto the elevator. He wanted Dani to defend herself, like she'd been doing with him. He wanted to take this woman down a peg for being such a bitch.

He moved into the elevator and put himself between Dani and the woman. The woman smiled at him, all coy sweetness. "You must be the new field operator. Mr. Knight and Mr. Blackwell always pick the best men." She held out her hand. "I'm Ashley."

He gave her his game face, the one he wore just before he made a kill. She blanched and withdrew her hand. He turned his back on her.

"You did great, Dani," he said. "Don't worry, you'll be off probation and a full operator in no time."

The woman behind him gasped. But Danika's tentative smile made his lie worth it.

While Jake drove Dani to her apartment he spoke on the phone with Rhys, who was going through her place, clearing it.

Dani kept quiet. She needed to figure out where she was going to stay tonight. She didn't have any close friends besides Tassia and Chuck, and Chuck lived in such a tiny apartment that she hated to impose on him.

It looked as if she'd have to use her meager savings and get a hotel room. Or maybe she could stay at E.D.G.E. Mike often slept there.

Jake pulled up to her apartment and found parking on the street, just as the sun's last light died. Rhys met them at the main entrance. "All clear," he said. "I'll watch from the street."

She went inside and Jake followed. At her door, he drew his pistol and motioned her to wait. He disappeared into her apartment, coming back long moments later.

"Okay, it's clear. Grab enough clothes for a week." He closed the door behind them and stood by it, like her personal sentinel.

She paused before heading to her room. "Thank you for helping me."

He nodded, his intense gaze searing her, before breaking eye contact. "Two minutes, remember."

Right. She headed for her bedroom. She started stripping out of the tracksuit and her grimy pajamas before she'd even closed her door. She pulled on her favorite jeans, tight but soft, a pair of boots, and a t-shirt with her leather jacket over it. Then she snagged her backpack from under her bed and shoved clothes into it. She made a quick pit stop in the bathroom, snagging toiletries, and eyed the shower longingly.

"Come on, Kashnikov," Jake said. "If they've got eyes on this place, our time's running out."

Hearing him say her real name made her pause. It had been too long since she'd heard someone say it. She smiled.

"Coming."

Jake's phone buzzed and he spoke briefly into it before turning back to her. "We've got company. We need to go out through the balcony."

"The balcony? Why not the stairs?" She couldn't scale a freaking building.

"I don't want a confrontation. You've been through enough. Let's just leave nice and quiet."

Jake moved fast, sliding open the glass door so it made no sound. She joined him outside, slipping her pack onto her back. The balcony was small, just large enough to hold her tiny grill, two chairs, and a dead potted plant. The wrought-iron railing was pretty, but fake, so it wouldn't rust. It was a classy building, after all.

Her neighbor's balcony was a large ten-foot leap away. Was she supposed to jump? Jake shut the door and smiled. "Don't look so worried. We're not going far."

"Not going far?" She looked over the side to the ground

four stories below.

Jake had already hopped over the railing and stood on the other side of it. His calm gaze assessing. "Down one, I think."

Her eyes widened, remembering hanging from the walkway just hours ago. "We're four floors up. Shouldn't we just hide?"

"We are. Just not in your apartment." He crouched down, grabbed the bottom edge of the concrete and flipped himself down and onto the balcony of her downstairs neighbor, not even giving her a chance to be irritated with him. He disappeared for a moment before he returned and extended his arms to her. "Your turn," he said.

She swung her legs over the railing and positioned her toes on the balcony edge. Jake had made it seem so easy. She tried to ignore the fact that she was four stories up, but she couldn't help looking down.

"Look at me, Dani." Jake's calm voice drew her gaze. "Place your hands on the lower bars. Then swing your legs down. Trust me. I've got you."

"Trust him, he says," she muttered to herself. She gripped where he'd said and noticed how slick her palms had become. "I don't know about this."

"Dani. Think of this as a test. You need to trust me."

"This isn't a freaking test; this is the Russian mafia out to kill me."

He sighed. "You are an exasperating woman."

She gripped the bars. "And you…" She swung her legs

down with a gasp. "Are an insufferable know-it-all." Her legs dangled for a fleeting second and her sweaty hands slipped. "Do you have me?" Her voice squeaked.

Warm arms came around her legs and his deep voice soothed her. "I have you. I'm not going to let you fall. Now let go."

She didn't want to. What if he slipped? It was an awkward angle and she wasn't a petite woman. What if he couldn't hold her?

"Dani," he whispered patiently.

He was a Navy SEAL, and she'd seen his biceps. He could handle her weight. She could trust in that. Her apartment door burst open. She didn't wait around to see who entered.

She let go.

Jake felt the added weight as Dani let go. He gripped her legs tight to his chest and slid his hands up to her firm ass. It fit so nicely in his palms that he had to restrain himself from kneading it. Despite the precarious situation, he felt himself harden. He lowered Dani slowly and soundlessly down his body, hugging her soft curves to his chest. She was panting by the time her breasts came within sight of his gaze. He held her like that, too high for her toes to touch the ground, and completely within his power. He smiled at the thought.

Her wicked tongue came out to lick her lips and his dick

strained against his jeans. The only things that stopped him from following that tongue back into her mouth were the two thugs in her apartment.

The balcony door slid open. He set Dani on her feet, holding her beside him, and focused completely on the task at hand.

They spoke Russian, and despite not being as fluent as Dani, he still knew enough to understand what they said.

"We missed her," one said. The scratch of a lighter sounded. "Vladimir won't be happy." Cigarette smoke wafted down to them.

"Don't worry. We'll find the bitch and pay her back for Petroff."

Jake felt the tremble go through Dani at the thug's words. He gave her a little squeeze. He pulled his gun from behind his back.

He wasn't going to let anything happen to this woman, who was such an odd mixture of scrappiness and vulnerability. Even now she lifted her chin, though her eyes still showed fear, and nodded at him. He gave her a last squeeze before motioning her back against the brick wall. He'd already checked the balcony door. It was locked, but he'd jimmy it in a minute. Right now, he wanted to hear more of what the two men said.

"No. Can't." The smoking man exhaled heavily. "Vladimir has decided she is to work for us."

"This is a lotta trouble for a whore."

"*Mudak*," the man swore. "She's some kind of computer

expert. He wants her skills." A slight wheezing laugh. "And her body."

"And if she doesn't want to?"

A small pause while the man exhaled again. "Then we get to have our fun."

Dammit. Jake did not like the sound of that. He wasn't letting Dani out of his sight until this was over.

The smallest whisk of sound behind him had him spinning toward the noise. Dani stood by the open balcony door with a shit-eating grin on her face. Silently, she waved him through the door.

The woman had serious skills. They hustled into the dark apartment and he slid the door quietly shut.

A well-used La-Z-Boy sat in front of a large, wall-mounted TV. A battered side table held a lamp and a pile of car and girly magazines. A heavily stained beige chair that looked to have been taken from a dumpster was the only other furniture in the small living area.

A growl behind him raised the hair on the back of his neck. He turned to see a large Rottweiler hunched low to the ground, its claws digging into the grayish carpet. It must have weighed about one-twenty.

He stepped in front of Dani. With his bigger mass, he'd be harder to take down. He needed to neutralize the dog before it made any noise to alert the men. Tensing his muscles, he waited for the dog to spring.

"It's just Bear," Dani said, sidestepping him and moving to the dog. Her voice changed to the one women used when they spoke to babies and puppies. "Come here, Bear. You're a good guard dog, aren't you?"

Bear started to wag his hind end and took a few steps toward Dani. Jake began to relax and turned to get a glimpse out the balcony door. Bear growled.

Jake froze.

Bear went back to wagging his tail and panting while Dani kept cooing and rubbing around his ears and neck.

Jake tested the dog and stepped toward the front door. Another skin-crawling growl sounded. "I don't think Bear likes me."

"He's just precious." Dani continued to pat the dog. "And his owner is a big goof, isn't he?"

"Are you expecting that dog to answer you?"

She glared at him over her shoulder and he had to stifle a laugh.

"We need to get out of here. Rhys is waiting."

She stood up and gave Bear a final pat. Jake started for the apartment door and Bear lunged at him. Jake managed to swat away the dog's head using a forearm strike to its nose. The dog whimpered and tucked its tail. Big coward.

Dani threw her arms around Bear's neck. "Easy, Jake. He's just doing his job."

"Should I have let him bite me?" Jake shook his head. "We don't have time for this. Hold the dog while I check the hallway." He went to the apartment door, keeping an eye on Bear the whole time. He didn't trust that Dani could hold the dog, if it decided to take revenge.

He unlocked the door and cracked it open. The hallway was quiet. "Say goodbye to the mutt," he said, stepping out. "It's time to go."

"Goodbye, Bear," she said, giving him a last ear rub. "I have to go with the big, bossy SEAL now." When she moved to Jake's side, he struggled not to laugh at her little rebellion.

They didn't speak as they left her neighbor's apartment and raced down the stairwell and out onto the street. In the dark, they could still see the glow of the thug's cigarette as he stood smoking on Dani's balcony. The other was probably tossing her place just for shits and giggles.

Rhys appeared out of the shadows near their car. "Everything good?"

Jake nodded. "Cakewalk."

"Good. Call if you need backup." He walked down the street to a black sedan and got in.

As soon as Jake pulled their car away from the curb, he glanced at Dani. "So, where are we staying tonight?"

CHAPTER 15

Dani choked at Jake's question and ended up coughing. His lips twitched, and she glared at him.

"You can't… You're not staying with me." Besides, she didn't know where she was staying.

"Wrong answer." Jake steered the car onto a busy street. "You need protection. I'm not leaving you alone until this is over."

Dani's chest tightened and she was pretty sure she was doing a good imitation of a fish when he sighed in exasperation. "Look, if you want, I can get someone else assigned to watch you." His fingers tightened on the wheel. "But you need *someone*."

Dani rubbed her forearm, feeling the buttery leather of her jacket. The thought of Koven or someone else looking after her, ordering her around, made her grimace. "You," she whispered, giving in. "I want you."

Jake's gaze seared her. She hastily rephrased. "I mean, you've got experience..." She huffed a breath. *Try again, Dani.* "You're good at this protection stuff, so yes, you'd be the best choice for me."

He snorted. "Okay, Dani," he said. "Where are we going?"

She shrugged. "How about the operator's lounge at E.D.G.E.?"

"Seriously?" he asked. "You don't have any friends who might let you bunk with them?"

She stared out into the darkness, noting they were headed toward downtown. "No."

He didn't say anything for a while. She wanted to smooth away the small furrow between his brows, but didn't know how, so she bit her lip and looked out the window.

Jake pulled the car into the underground parking of a large chain hotel.

Dani straightened in her seat. "What are we doing?"

Jake didn't look at her. "We need showers. You need real food and a bed, not vending machines and a crappy couch. This is the hotel I'm staying at." His lips compressed and he looked at her. "Deal with it."

Her eyebrows rose. Deal with it? She shrugged. "Real food sounds good to me."

He nodded, and didn't say anything while he parked the

car. "You do know you'll be staying in my room with me, right?"

"Wait. What?"

He snorted. "Don't worry," he said. "You can have the bed. I'll take the floor."

For a moment she wondered what Jake slept in. She squashed that thought. She was in so much trouble.

"I'll take the floor," she said finally, as they took the elevator up. "It's your room. But you have to buy me dinner."

"You'll take the bed. And E.D.G.E. is buying us both dinner." Jake opened the door to his room. "Make yourself at home. Rhys is right across the hall. I'm going to update him."

The room housed a king-sized bed, a TV almost as large, an elegant wooden desk, and a table for two. She walked past the bed with its creamy duvet, straight to the window and opened the curtains. Seeing the street below made her feel better.

She just wasn't used to being around strangers that much, let alone a stranger who happened to be a gorgeous man who'd already kissed her. She swallowed. *Dangerous thoughts, Dani.*

The door closed behind her with a thunk and she jumped. Jake moved past her, giving her plenty of space. He closed the curtains she'd just opened. "Sorry," he said. "Can't have people seeing in here."

"Right. Of course." She shook herself mentally. She was being ridiculous. Jake had already said that he wouldn't pursue anything with her because they were working together.

But she also remembered his other statement about wanting to do delicious things to her. She wondered what those things might be.

"Dani?"

She jumped. "Yes?"

His eyes held a slight twinkle, as if he liked making her nervous. "I asked if you were hungry."

Yes, she thought. *Hungry for you.* Her face reddened and she looked away, pulling her pack off and then grabbing the room-service menu. "Um, sure."

The silence that followed pressured her to look at him, but she kept her head down and flipped the pages of the menu. Finally he moved away.

"I think I'll have the chicken salad," she said.

"How about I order while you use the shower first? The food should be here by the time you're done."

She nodded and escaped into the bathroom. Twenty minutes later, she left the bathroom refreshed and in control. She'd left her hair damp but combed, and trailing down the back of her t-shirt. She'd put her jeans back on. In her haste to pack, she hadn't grabbed the boxers she usually slept in. She wasn't planning on wearing her jeans to bed, but she wasn't going to parade around in her thong either.

Jake sat on the bed, his back against the headboard while he watched hockey on TV. Spring meant the playoffs. "Do you follow hockey?" she asked.

Jake shrugged. "I love watching any sport. I don't usually have a lot of time to watch TV though, so this is nice."

She took a breath and casually sat on the far side of the bed, leaning back against the headboard like he had. He glanced at her once, but didn't say anything. Watching the game lulled her and her muscles began to relax.

Someone knocked on the door. A pistol appeared in Jake's hand and he checked who it was. He slid the weapon under his shirt before opening the door to the hotel waiter. After signing the check, he closed the door on the waiter and wheeled the cart to the table.

"What did you order?" she asked.

"Steak for myself," he said, lifting the lid on the tray. He grinned. "They had *poutine*, so I ordered that as well, and a beer for you." He handed her the beer and then started putting the food on the table.

"Come join me," he said.

Dani hesitated only a moment before sitting across from him. He started on the steak and she pushed the *poutine* over to him after she saw him eyeing it. He smiled and started in on it too. She picked at the chicken salad, watching him eat, sipping the beer. He drank only water.

He rubbed his thigh under the table.

"Is your leg hurting you?"

His hand stopped rubbing. "It's fine." He continued eating and didn't look at her. And suddenly she wanted to know more about the man sitting across from her. This warrior who put himself in danger regularly, who offered to put himself in danger for her.

"What happened to your leg?"

If she hadn't been watching him so closely she wouldn't have seen his hesitation.

"Bullet."

"When?" Two could play at the monosyllabic game, she thought.

He sighed and sat back. "On a mission last year. I can't tell you the details."

He was so defensive that she couldn't help probing more. "How long did it take for you to recover?"

His face tightened and he sawed at his steak. She thought he was going to ignore this question too, but he finally responded. "I'm still recovering. The docs don't think I'll gain full function back, but I'm proving them wrong."

He didn't look at her as he said this, so she decided to dig somewhere else. "Why'd you become a SEAL?"

Again he didn't look at her. "Would you believe because I'm patriotic?"

"You're not really open about your life, are you, Jake?"

He smirked and pointed at her. "Pot." He pointed at himself. "Kettle. Black."

She laughed. "Point for you."

"Didn't realize this was a competition."

Her smile disappeared. "It's not." She ate a piece of chicken. It had a Thai peanut sauce that made her want to gobble the whole thing. "I'm just trying to get to know you better. You know, since we're spending the night together."

Her face heated at what her words implied. She bent her head and concentrated on cutting up her chicken. She could feel the weight of his stare, but she refused to acknowledge it.

Finally he sighed. "I had just graduated college when I decided to join the Navy."

"Which is why Rhys calls you College."

He nodded.

"So, why'd you join the Navy? Why not a cushy job somewhere?"

He rolled his shoulders once and then looked at his plate, pushing a lonely bite of steak around. "One night I was walking my girlfriend home across campus, and we got mugged."

Her eyebrows rose. Who'd be dumb enough to mug Jake? "Did you obliterate the guy?"

He looked away. "No…I let my fear control me. I handed over my money like I was told."

She sat back. She just couldn't picture it, some guy getting the jump on Jake. She could see the memory tore at him. "Did the guy have a knife?"

"A gun." He ate the bite of steak, his shoulders hunched slightly. She watched him for a moment, thinking about a young man with no experience with violence being held at gunpoint.

"Had you ever even been in a fight before?"

"Some scrapes."

She huffed a breath. "So you're beating yourself up

because you didn't stop an armed assailant when you were untrained? I've dealt with drugged-up street thugs and they're unpredictable and very scary. I'd say you were smart to hand over your money, or you wouldn't be here protecting me right now."

Jake's gray eyes were dark. "That's not what my girlfriend thought."

"What?"

He sat back in his chair and she could see his jaw set. "She called me a coward, and said a real man wouldn't just give in." He took a deep breath and released it. "From that moment, I promised myself I'd never let fear rule me again. So I joined the Navy and then the Teams."

She felt her eyebrows rise. "So you've never been scared since?"

He laughed. "No. I'm saying that even though I've been scared on missions, it doesn't control me."

Dani shook her head. "Well, I'm glad you joined the Navy and ended up here, but just so you know, your girlfriend was whacked. In that situation a 'real man' would be dead. Trust me," she said.

Then she grinned to lighten the mood. "You didn't date the smartest women back then, did you? Let me guess. Blonde with big boobs."

His lips twisted, but his eyes twinkled. "You may be right."

"I generally am," she said, waving a forkful of chicken at him before plopping it in her mouth.

He huffed a small laugh, but didn't reply. They ate in companionable silence for the rest of the meal. When he rubbed his thigh again, she couldn't hold her curiosity back.

"So how long until you're a SEAL again?"

He froze. "I'm still a SEAL." His voice was a granite growl. "My leg is fine."

She held up her hands. "I wasn't asking about your leg. I was just wondering if you'll be taking the job with E.D.G.E."

He shed his anger like a dog shaking water from its coat. "No," he said, turning back to his food. "I'm sorry. I belong with my team."

She nodded her head, even though he didn't see it. He was leaving soon, and for some reason she couldn't speak, her throat too tight for words. She gulped at her beer to ease the constriction.

"No need to be sorry," she said, pushing her plate away.

He stood up. "I'm gonna grab a shower," he said. "Why don't you head to bed? Don't wait for me."

He strode into the bathroom and shut the door. She slumped in her chair for a moment before straightening. Jake's answer had been so quick, as though he'd never even considered the E.D.G.E. offer.

Too bad, he'd make a great operator.

He'd also make a great lover, but he obviously wasn't interested. So she'd better just get some sleep.

She stripped off her jeans and got under the covers, but her skin felt too tight, so she left the game on to take her mind off things. The Oilers were kicking the Rangers' butts.

"Who's winning?" Jake's voice came from the open bathroom door.

"The Oil—" *Holy crap.* Jake only wore a towel. It hung low on his hips, showcasing ridges of muscle that begged for her touch. A small trail of hair below his navel led her eyes down until it disappeared under the towel.

"Sorry," he said, breaking her stare by moving past her. "I forgot my bag." He grabbed a black duffel from the top of the desk and went back to the bathroom.

Dani's breath left her body in a long, drawn-out exhale. "*Merde*, that was awkward," she muttered. And it proved Jake didn't see her as anything but a job, someone he'd been ordered to protect.

Okay, that was fine, she lied to herself. It was actually a good thing. Maybe the kiss at her place had been a complete mistake on his part. She didn't need to make him feel any more awkward. So no more staring.

In fact, he might as well have the other half of this massive bed. It wasn't as if they'd accidentally touch each other or anything.

Jake came back into the room wearing boxers and a black t-shirt. He opened the closet by the door and began taking the extra blanket and pillow out.

"Stop," she said. "This bed is huge and it's a tad ridiculous to make you sleep on the floor. Just take the other side."

He froze and didn't look at her. "I don't think that's a good idea."

"Look, I know I've been jumpy, but it's okay." She sighed. "I promise I won't force myself on you."

He faced her and the molten silver of his eyes took her breath away. "I'm not worried about *you*." His deep voice tugged at things inside her.

She swallowed. The safe choice would be to look away, turn off the light, and let Jake sleep on the floor. She took a deep breath and swung her feet from under the covers to the floor. She'd been making the safe choice for years and look where it'd gotten her. No friends and no life. She was tired of safe.

She stood up.

He set the blanket and pillow on the bed, head turned as if he wanted to look away, but his eyes stayed glued on her. She smiled and moved toward him, feeling secure in herself for the first time that evening. She stopped when she was a foot from him.

"Dani?" he said. Barely restrained power emanated from him, almost physically brushing over her sensitive skin. She wanted more.

She pulled off her t-shirt and stood before him. Her body was toned and her breasts were high, if not overly large.

She arched a brow at him.

He tore off his t-shirt and threw it to the ground, reaching out and grabbing her to him. His mouth ground against hers and she reveled in it. Her hands wound around his neck, pulling him closer.

Her breasts rubbed against his chest, the small amount

of hair there electrifying her as her nipples hardened. His tongue demanded entrance and she granted it, brimming with sensation as his hands roamed the skin of her back and pressed her hips against him. He was thick and long and very hard against her stomach.

The feel of his hot skin against her made her squeeze her legs together, even as she pressed herself closer, unable to stop herself from rubbing her breasts on his chest.

He groaned and his hand slid around a breast, lifting it and tugging the nipple until she gasped. Then he switched to the other one and her breath came short and sharp.

"Damn, you're beautiful," he said, his voice guttural. "I've been dreaming of this since I saw you fighting in the ring."

He bent down and lifted her into his arms. She hung onto his neck as he walked around the bed and laid her on it, his gaze never leaving hers. "Are you sure, Dani?"

"More than anything." It was true. She hadn't wanted anything so much in a long time. She hadn't allowed herself to want, to need, to desire, thinking that she was protecting herself. It was time to change.

She lifted her arms. "Come to me."

He slid into bed and covered her with his exquisite weight as he settled between her legs. She lifted her hips instinctively.

"Impatient?" He smiled.

She lifted her hips again, this time in demand, rubbing against him as he sucked in a breath. She held his gaze. "Yes."

His kiss ravaged her and she welcomed it, losing herself in the heat of her need. He pulled back. "The good things in life are worth waiting for." Then he slid down her body, pausing at her breasts. "Gorgeous." His mouth closed over one nipple and sucked hard. Her back arched and she cried out. Her breasts felt tight, seeming to swell from his touch. He laved the nipple and then switched to the other one. Her hands dug into his short hair, pressing him closer as she writhed beneath him.

"Time for more fun," he said and he slid her black thong down her legs. He stared at her for a moment, his eyes silver with heat, and she shivered. He smiled slowly, like a man who had discovered an unexpected treasure, and kissed her navel. He trailed his lips lower, closer to the place she wanted him to be. Her body shivered with desire.

But he veered down her leg and kissed her inner thigh. She almost moaned her disappointment, but he pushed her legs open farther and moved between them. Her heart thundered and when he finally lowered his hot mouth, she arched and sighed.

His tongue was rough and wet, the contrast sending her thoughts scattering. He licked and nibbled, and then added his fingers to the mix. They swirled lower, circling her entrance. Her hips bucked against him uncontrollably. He suckled on her sensitive bud, while his finger swept through her wet folds and pressed into her. Her insides tightened, a vast pressure loomed.

"More," she cried. "Please!"

He added a second finger and then pressed down with his tongue.

She screamed as the orgasm swept over her, tightening all her muscles as spasm after spasm rocked her, until eventually it released her, spent and limp.

She opened her eyes to see Jake had moved up her body and now smiled smugly at her. She let him be smug. He deserved it.

She smiled back. "Wow."

"That's only round one," he said, kissing her neck and trailing his lips up toward her ear.

"I'm always up for another round," she said, arching her neck and giving him access. He took it, nuzzling her skin and finding the place behind her ear that had her lower belly clenching.

"Ah," he said, nuzzling the skin again as she arched into him. "There's a spot I need to remember."

Her hands ran up his chest, skimming over every ridge of muscle and then down his broad back, wondering how this man, this warrior, could be here with her. She clutched at him as he licked at that spot and desire once again shot through her.

He pulled back for a moment. "Protection," he said and left the bed to rummage in his bag, coming back moments later with a condom. He ripped it out of the package and she took it from him, seeing her opportunity to tease him a little.

She pushed him back on the bed so his powerful body

lay waiting for her. The scar on his leg was a testament to his strength and dedication. She trailed her fingers down it before kissing it slowly. His eyes clouded.

She turned her attention higher. His arousal stood out from his body, strong and thick. She ran a finger down its length and Jake sucked in a breath.

This was for her. She knelt over him, leaning down to use her tongue where her finger had just gone. His chest rose as he inhaled deeply, and his hands fisted in the sheets.

She licked him again, teasing, enjoying how she could make him writhe for her.

"Dani," he growled.

She smiled and engulfed him in her mouth. His hips lifted and he groaned. The slight salty taste of him encouraged her to suck harder. His hands tangled in her hair as she used her tongue against the sensitive underside.

He pulled her off him. "You make me lose control."

"Good." She licked her lips and his eyes tracked the movement. She took the condom and rolled it over him slowly, enjoying his groans.

"Enough," he said and abruptly rolled her beneath him.

Her eyes widened when he shifted and his cock nudged her entrance. His kiss claimed her and she whimpered. Her legs opened farther in invitation, but Jake waited, kissing her as if he had all the time in the world. He held himself above her with one arm while his other hand played with her breasts, rubbing his thumb back and forth across her nipples until she twisted uncontrollably beneath him.

Wetness soaked her legs. He licked the spot behind her ear and her breath shuddered from her. She drowned in sensation, his lips on her neck, his hands on her body and his swollen hardness rubbing between her legs. He pulled back and looked at her.

"I think you're ready now," he said darkly.

The heat of his body scorched her as he pushed steadily into her. She panted as her swollen tissues stretched to accommodate him. Her eyes drifted shut.

"Look at me, Dani," Jake said. His gaze captured hers, not releasing it as he sank in to the hilt. He slowly pulled back and then plunged forward. Her hands clutched at his back, digging into the muscle there, desperate to get closer.

A rhythm built between them, faster and harder, their breaths mingling. The tide of pleasure surged inside her, tightening everything in its wake, until her orgasm exploded. Her world went white as she strained against Jake.

Jake shouted and then plunged deep inside her, grinding against her core, setting off another round of spasms.

A long while later, when her heart beat normally, Jake turned off the lights and pulled her into the circle of his arms. He kissed her neck lightly and she shivered. He pulled the blankets over them and hugged her close.

"Sleep," he said. "I've got you."

CHAPTER 16

The next morning, Jake showered and threw on a pair of jeans. He came out of the bathroom to see the morning sun peeking around the edges of the hotel curtain. Dani lay sprawled on the bed, her dark silky hair over her face as she slept. He grinned, thinking about how he'd tired her out last night and again this morning.

He rubbed a towel over his damp hair as he shifted a curtain aside. Rush-hour traffic on the street and sidewalks greeted him. Being eight stories up barely muffled the honks and growls of the cars below. It could be any street in any big city. His gaze lifted and the "Mountain" west of downtown reminded him this wasn't just any city.

"Don't you ever sleep?" Dani's voice was groggy.

He turned to her and shrugged. "I don't need much," he said. "I'll order room service while you grab a shower."

She ducked her head under the pillow. "What if I don't want to get up?"

He moved to the bed and, unable to help himself, trailed a hand down her arm, feeling the silky smoothness of her skin, remembering her taste. She lifted the pillow from her head and her kissable lips parted. His cock hardened.

"Now I really don't want to get up," she said, her voice husky.

"You have to." He swallowed and forced his hand away. "Briefing this morning." He backed away, picked up the phone, and ordered food, he wasn't sure what.

She watched him from under lowered lids, her green eyes dark, and licked her lips. He lowered the phone and sat beside her on the bed. He stroked his hands up her arms and then down her chest, taking the sheet with him. Her golden skin felt like warm velvet under his hands. She gasped when he tweaked a nipple. He loved the sounds he could draw from her.

"We have to wait for the food anyway," he said, lowering his head.

Dani enjoyed the latte Jake had gotten her while he drove them to the E.D.G.E. offices. As they approached, he turned sharply right, to an entrance Dani had never seen used. He stopped the car before the metal door. A small control pad stood beside his window. He pressed his thumb on the pad and the door rolled up.

"Huh," Dani said, sipping her coffee. "I never knew we had our own parking."

Jake smiled. "It's only for the operators and top brass. The range is down here too."

"Range?"

"E.D.G.E. has a lot of nifty toys, and many more underground floors." He gave her a glance before maneuvering into a parking spot. "Have you ever shot a gun before?"

"A couple of times," Dani said. "I'm not fond of them."

Jake nodded. "They're not for everyone. But if you're serious about being an operator, then we should get you up to speed."

She shook her head. "I don't think I can become an operator. I don't have the military background or training that seems to be needed. And even if I did, I'm not sure I'm cut out for it."

"You handle yourself well under pressure and you have useful skills. You don't need to be in the field to help, Dani. You could be IT or comms support on missions. Mike doesn't have a military background."

IT or comms support. Yes, she could do those jobs. She smiled slowly as her future started to look a little brighter and a whole lot more interesting. Maybe she would have a chance to do something good with her life after all.

"Come on," Jake said. "The briefing started five minutes ago."

Upstairs, they headed straight for the war room. Chuck, Rhys, Koven, and two other operators, a man and a woman she didn't know, sat around the table. Derrick Blackwell stood in front of them with his arms crossed.

"You're late," Blackwell said.

Jake stood beside her, his shoulder touching hers. "Sorry, sir, I—"

"It's my fault," Dani piped in. She held up her coffee. "I needed a latte." She didn't mention that it wasn't the latte that had made them late.

Blackwell's gaze narrowed. For a moment panic seized her. Did they all know that she'd slept with Jake?

She flushed. *Seriously, Dani,* she berated herself. *How could they know?* She needed to breathe and control her red face, or it wouldn't be long before they clued in.

But if it wasn't that, then what? There was a distinct air of tension in the room. Chuck looked up from where he'd been staring at his hands. Some emotion she couldn't read flickered in his eyes. "I'm glad you're okay, kid."

She nodded. He didn't seem that glad. None of them did. Chuck turned away and refused to look at her again. Her stomach rolled over when she realized no one was looking at them. Well, her, anyway. Rhys nodded at Jake and she saw his lips firm. That couldn't be good.

"Sitrep," Blackwell said.

Jake stepped forward. "Two of Rusakov's men entered

Everett's apartment last night. They didn't see us. We overheard them talking. Apparently, Vladimir wants her to work for him."

Blackwell arched a brow. "I assume you've taken care of protection for her."

"Yes, sir," Jake said. "It's covered."

Blackwell nodded. "Good. Now, Ms. Everett…or would you prefer to be called Ms. Kashnikov?"

Dani's blood drained from her face. He knew. In fact, none of them seemed surprised at the use of her real name. They all knew. She swallowed against her suddenly dry throat. "Either is fine."

"Well, Ms. Kashnikov, please hand over your passkey to Lieutenant Harrison and listen to everything he tells you. Your life may depend on it. We'll talk more after the briefing." He looked at Jake. "Escort her to the fifth floor and we'll finish the briefing when you return."

Dani frowned. Hand over her passkey? That meant she no longer had access to any of the operator floors. The fifth floor was where all the civilians worked. "I don't understand," she said. "Aren't I helping with this case?"

Blackwell looked up, his icy eyes pinning her. He obviously wasn't used to anyone questioning him.

"No."

"Why not?"

Blackwell drew himself upright and crossed his arms. "Unfortunately, Ms. Kashnikov, in light of your performance recently, I'm unsure whether you're fit to be a team member or even to continue working at E.D.G.E."

Chuck made a strangled noise, but quieted under Blackwell's glare.

"My performance?" Her voice rose on the last note. "Are you referring to me being kidnapped? How is that my fault?"

Blackwell's voice got softer and colder. "Not the kidnapping. Rather, it's the information you failed to provide to E.D.G.E. I know your background, Ms. Kashnikov—that you used to work for the Rusakovs and, in particular, that you were rather *intimately* associated with Vladimir Rusakov.

"The issue I have with you isn't that your ex-boyfriend is under investigation, but that we didn't learn this information from *you*. You've had the opportunity to trust us as we've trusted you, and yet you chose again and again not to."

"But—" Dani said.

Blackwell held up a hand. "Did you read secure files on the E.D.G.E. database? Did you attempt an illegal and unsupervised hack from one of E.D.G.E.'s computers? Did you break and enter a building under E.D.G.E. surveillance in order to secure information that E.D.G.E. needed, but then didn't offer up that information until you'd been caught in the act?"

Dani's insides twisted. "Yes."

"At least you're being honest with us now," he said. Then he sighed. "Until I know that I can absolutely trust you, I need you off this team. I don't have time to second-guess whether anyone working for me is sharing all their information with me."

Only years of keeping her face impassive let her stand still while it felt like he ripped off layers of her clothes and exposed her naked, cold body to the world. She wanted to hunch and shiver as shame washed over her.

He knew everything. From her twisted relationship with Vladimir, to every mistake she'd made since this whole mess had started. But it was the way he revealed her past with Vladimir that made her want to hide.

How had Blackwell found out? Chuck knew her past, but he'd never tell that particular secret. No one else knew about her relationship with Vladimir.

Her insides turned to ice. No one except Jake.

She turned to him and his jaw clenched, but otherwise he didn't react. Had it all been a lie? Had he been playing her this whole time for information? God, had he slept with her to see if she had anything else incriminating to say?

She tore her gaze from his and backed toward the door. She felt hemmed in by Blackwell's critical gaze and the operators' sidelong glances.

Arguing would be useless. Blackwell had already turned away. She compressed her lips to stop them from trembling, squared her shoulders, and left the room.

She could hear raised voices behind her and wondered if only Chuck had her back. Did they all condemn her? Part of her wanted to run, far and fast, but she shook her head.

Tassia was the important one. She had to stay, even if she could only help out with information. She'd do everything possible to rescue Tassia.

And then she'd leave. She'd take her savings and find somewhere new to settle and someone new to be.

A footstep behind her alerted her to his presence. "Get away from me, Jake."

"Dani, wait." He touched her arm.

She spun toward him, flinging off his touch. "No. I can't believe you told them what I said. Why would you do that?"

"I'm sorry. They needed to know. I believe Vladimir has a personal grudge against you and he seems obsessed. I didn't realize Blackwell would drop you from the team. I don't think it's your past he holds against you. None of the rest of us do."

"Oh, really? You don't hold it against me, but you don't actually trust me, either." Her fists clenched, trying to hold it together. "How long have you known about my past, Jake? You knew before we talked at my place, didn't you?"

Jake held up his hands. "I suspected you had a shady past. You have a file, but I didn't have access. I spoke with you that night because I needed to know everything in order to protect you. And I wanted you to tell me yourself. I wanted you to trust me. Without that, we couldn't work together in the future."

"You did this so we could work together," she said, her voice carefully even. His admission deflated her anger, leaving her drained. Did he only see her as a colleague?

"Why did you sleep with me?" Had she really asked that? Her life was crumbling, but somehow that was the question that had escaped. And now that it had, she wanted it answered.

"Dani, don't do this." Jake ran a hand over his buzzed head. "We don't have time to talk about this now. I have to get back to the briefing."

"Right. Of course." Tassia took priority. Her shoulders slumped. She handed over her passkey, but looked away from Jake's compassionate gaze. "I'm going to the fifth-floor lounge. Let me know when there's something I'm allowed to help with."

"Dani, we'll talk later. Okay?" Jake said.

"Sure." Dani walked to the elevator, knowing Jake watched her but refusing to look back. She couldn't bear to see the pity in his eyes.

In the lounge, she dropped her pack to the floor and flopped into one of the easy chairs.

Merde. She'd really screwed up this time. Chuck had told her from the beginning she should tell them the truth. And now it was too late. They would never trust her now.

Shame washed over her. Why couldn't she have owned up to who she had once been? If she had, then maybe she wouldn't be in this mess now. She'd been a stupid, lonely kid who'd fallen for the wrong guy. A guy who had turned out to be dangerous and psychotic. She shivered and hugged herself.

Her happiness this morning seemed so long ago. She

sighed and grabbed her pack. Even if she was no longer welcome in IT, at least she could go over Dmitri's files on her laptop. Perhaps she could find a clue to where Tassia might be.

Her cell rang and she dug it out of her pack. The number was unavailable and her heart started to beat faster. "Hello?" she said.

"*Bonjour*, Danika," Vladimir purred into her ear. "We need to talk. Is there anyone else listening?"

She hesitated. "No."

"Good. I want to make a deal with you," he said. "I will let your friend go, if you come back to me."

Dani froze. Go back? "To do what?"

"Doing what you do best, *Kotyonok*. We could use your help with our exports."

"I won't help you traffic innocent women."

He chuckled. "I'd forgotten how soft you are. Don't worry, *Kotyonok*. These women aren't innocent. Most of them signed on willingly."

Dani doubted that. "I still won't work for you."

Vladimir sighed heavily. "Then I'm sorry about your friend."

"What are you going to do?"

"Kill her, of course."

"Wait!" Dani shouted, afraid Vladimir would hang up the phone.

"Yes?" he said calmly.

She gritted her teeth. "Where should I meet you?"

She had five minutes, tops, before she had to be on the road. Vladimir had only given her twenty minutes to get to the drop site across town. She debated for less than a second about what her next move would be. She ran for the stairs to go to the sixth floor to find Jake.

The door wouldn't open.

Merde! It was locked and she'd given up her passkey.

Her insides twisted with the realization. She couldn't get upstairs to the people who could help. She'd been locked out of the inner circles of E.D.G.E. She'd have time later to think about what that meant for her. Right now she had to help Tass.

She yanked out her cell and called Jake. It went straight to voicemail. She left him as many details as possible before taking the elevator to the parking garage. She jimmied the lock on Jake's E.D.G.E. car and hotwired it.

She had fifteen minutes.

The morning sunshine promised a beautiful day as Dani pulled the sedan into the parking lot behind the three-story brick building on the north end of the island. It was close to midday, but the area looked deserted. One window at the back was boarded up, another clearly had

had something thrown through it, and the brick wall had gang tags spraypainted all over it. A wooden chair propped open the back door.

She got out of the car, leaving it running, and strode to the door, her pack on her back. Inside, she came face to barrel with a Glock held by a thick man in jeans and a cheap leather jacket that creaked when he moved.

"Danika?" His Russian accent sharpened her name like a whetstone.

"*Da*. Take me to Vladimir." She spoke Russian to emphasize she belonged.

He lowered his pistol. "Follow me."

Vladimir stood in the open area of the building's first floor, the front windows behind him, a welcoming smile on his face. Two of his men stood nearby. One held Tassia with an arm around her throat and a gun at her temple.

One eye was swollen shut and she clutched her arm against her chest as if it hurt. She wore no shoes or coat. Dani barely recognized Tassia's favorite silk sheath dress, hanging filthy and torn on her shaking frame.

"Tassia?" Dani didn't know what she was asking, but the state of her friend made her fear what she'd been through.

"You shouldn't have come, Dani," she said, her voice hoarse. "They're monsters."

The man holding Tassia jerked her back against him and whispered something in her ear. She paled further and her good hand scratched at his arm.

Dani pressed her lips together. She would see these men

dead. "Leave her alone," she barked in Russian.

Vladimir chuckled. "You do not give orders here, *Kotyonok*. But I'm glad for your friend's sake that you were so prompt."

"Let her go," Dani said coldly.

Vladimir's smile disappeared.

Dani stood her ground and hardened her voice. She would not waver before Vladimir, or he'd pounce on any weakness he found. "Let Tassia go and I'll come with you, like we agreed."

Vladimir's beautiful face twisted. "Why don't I keep her and use her as leverage against you?"

Dani sighed as if she were bored of the conversation, even though her heart raced and she had to keep her hands in her pockets so no one would see them tremble. "Vladimir, you don't need her. The authorities are searching everywhere for her. I'm sure Dmitri doesn't like the extra attention you've brought to the family business."

He took a step toward her, his hands clenched into fists. "Do not threaten me with my father, or no matter our history, I will make you regret it."

She smiled just a little. She almost had him. "I'm not threatening you, Vlad. I'm advising you. Just like I used to."

Vladimir's hands unclenched, but his eyes remained narrowed. He looked like a predatory angel. "Do not think that I trust you, Danika. But I keep my word." He turned to his men. "Release her."

The man holding Tassia gave her a push, so she ended

up stumbling toward Dani. Dani caught her and held her against her side.

Vladimir spoke in English. "It was lovely to meet you, Tassia. You have two minutes before my men start hunting you." He eyed his watch. "Time starts now."

"Dani?" Tassia's nails dug into her forearms.

"Black sedan outside," Dani whispered to her. "It's running."

She stared at Dani, unmoving. Vladimir started to grin.

"Run," Dani barked. And Tassia did.

She waited, muscles tight, while Vladimir glanced at his watch, before looking up and giving her a smug grin. "I'm bored," he said to his men. "Kill the woman."

His men took off running.

"That wasn't two minutes," Dani protested.

He shrugged. "I lied."

Dani licked her lips. It was only her and Vladimir at the moment. She was strong and fast. He didn't seem to be armed. Maybe she could outrun him.

He tutted and pouted those full lips. "Don't think you can back out of our deal, *Kotyonok*. I have men stationed outside with orders to kill you if you appear without me."

A gunshot sounded, then a car engine roared and tires squealed. Dani felt her shoulders loosen. Tassia had gotten away. At least something had gone right.

Vladimir scowled when his men returned empty-handed. "*Blyad*. Clear the place out."

"*Da*. We're on it, Mr. Rusakov."

Dani arched a brow. "Mister?"

"Don't irritate me, Danika," Vladimir said. "I'm not the man you left five years ago."

No, he was crazier and meaner than the man she'd run from. But she didn't say that. Instead, she smiled at him. She needed to keep him off-balance, and make him remember their relationship. Maybe she could get him to trust her again, at least enough that she could escape.

And this time she would run far from Montreal and Vladimir and the Rusakov family. A small part of her acknowledged that she'd also be running far from E.D.G.E., and from Jake.

CHAPTER 17

The trunk opened and she squinted against the light someone shone into her eyes. Her stomach grumbled and she scowled, hiding her fear behind anger. The gag in her mouth made her throat dry and her shoulders ached from having her hands tied behind her back. She'd been in the trunk of Vladimir's car since about noon, when the Boulder Brothers had tied her up and chucked her in. Beyond the flashlight, darkness waited.

Of course, Ivan and Boris hadn't taken all afternoon to drive her around. They'd parked the car at one point and left her tied in the trunk. From the jokes they made afterward, they'd gone for dinner while she'd tired herself out attempting to kick the trunk open.

The men now hauled her out by her aching arms and set her on her feet. The well-kept farmhouse in front of them looked as though it held a loving family, complete with a golden retriever. A large, lit barn stood about fifty meters away, with several outbuildings arranged around it. She couldn't see any other farms or houses close by.

Vladimir stepped into view. He pulled the gag from her mouth. "Tomorrow you will start to work for us."

The way his gaze slithered over her body made her insides shrivel.

"And tonight?" she asked, hating that her voice trembled.

He smiled, but his voice and eyes were cold. "Tonight, I punish you for running from me, and teach you what happens if you ever do it again."

She exhaled hard, as if she'd been punched. His smile widened. He liked seeing her at his mercy and scared. She couldn't show him any fear, or it would set him and his sadistic tendencies off. She made her face as cold as his and shrugged as much as she was able. "Whatever gives you your jollies."

He slapped her hard and pain splintered along her jaw.

"You should be more respectful, you don't have your boyfriend to protect you," he said.

She pulled herself straight. "I don't have a boyfriend, and I don't need anyone's protection."

He laughed. "Have you looked around, *Kotyonok*? You need my protection. I run things here." He looked at the Boulder Brothers. "Bring her."

He strode to one of the outbuildings and the brothers grabbed her arms in bruising grips and hauled her along. She tried to shrug them off.

"Vladimir, is this really necessary? I kept my end of the deal. I came when you called and asked me to work with you."

"Not with. *For.*" He didn't turn or pause in his stride.

The outbuilding was about the size of a two-car garage and made of wood that might have been painted brown, but it was hard to tell in the dark. The door creaked open and Vladimir hit the lights.

She sucked in a breath. It was one large room, open and empty except for various rusting tools lining the walls and a wooden straight-backed chair sitting in the middle of the concrete floor, right beside a drain. A single uncovered bulb hanging from the ceiling provided harsh light and showcased the dark stains surrounding the drain.

She shuddered and started to struggle, stomping on Boris's foot and kicking Ivan in the knee. She ran.

She hadn't taken more than ten steps when strong arms swooped her up and off her feet. Vladimir grinned at her. "I love your fire, *Kotyonok.*"

She wanted to spit in his face, but that would only make her punishment longer and harder. Instead she grinned back, making herself relax in his arms.

"I know you do," she said. Then she gave a little pout. "Are you really going to go through with this? You know you don't really want to."

"You know me too well, Danika." He lowered her so he held her chest to his with her toes only barely touching the ground. With her hands still tied behind her back, her breasts pressed against his muscled chest. She suppressed a shudder of revulsion as he purposely rubbed against her.

She deserved an acting trophy after this night. That is, if she survived.

He held her gaze as his hand tangled in her braid and gripped it tight. He lowered his mouth to hers and she forced herself not to struggle. He ravaged her mouth and nausea rose as his tongue thrust inside and dueled with hers.

His eyes glittered and he panted when he finally lifted his head. "I'm not sure I'm ever going to untie you," he said. Then he chuckled. "I like the fear I see in your eyes. It makes me hard."

She swallowed and put another layer of ice around her heart. If she didn't, she'd never survive. She had to return to the girl she used to be. There would be time later to mourn the loss of the person she'd been trying to become.

She tossed her head to loosen Vladimir's hand and gave him a haughty look. "I am not easy, and I don't take kindly to being forced. If you want me, then you're going to have to work for it."

His nostrils flared and for a moment she thought she'd pushed him too far, but then he flung his head back and laughed. She hoped no one saw her shudder.

"Ah, *Kotyonok*, you are funny." He released her and

turned to the Boulder Brothers. The one she'd kicked in the knee limped toward them and glared at her. "Tell Anya we have a guest, and see she is placed in the blue bedroom." He turned back to Dani. "I have business, Danika. I hope to see you later."

A chill ran through her at his words, but she only nodded her head.

With muted snarls, the Boulder Brothers led her into the farmhouse, which was decorated in a mix of sleek leather furniture and rough wooden tables. A deer's head with a full rack of antlers hung from the living room wall above a river-rock fireplace. The other wall was floor-to-ceiling windows, and she was sure the view would be of something beautiful come morning. The whole place had the feel of an elegant mountain lodge.

An elegant, isolated mountain lodge.

An open staircase led to a loft balcony and Ivan prodded her up the stairs and down a hall. Boris opened a door to reveal blue walls and a king-sized bed covered in a creamy duvet. Her backpack already sat in the middle of the bed. The snick of a knife leaving a sheath made her stiffen, but Ivan only used it to slice through the zip ties around her wrists.

She couldn't stop the groan that escaped when her arms swung forward to their normal position.

A hard shove sent her sprawling into the room. "*Sooka*," muttered Ivan, calling her a bitch. "When he tires of you, you'll pay for kicking me."

They shut the door and locked it. At least she was alone. She jumped up and immediately went to the window. Nailed shut.

She slammed her palms against the glass and it barely rattled in its frame. She pounded on it again and again. Nothing.

There was a small writing desk and chair in the room. She picked up the chair and slung it at the window. It bounced off. She wasn't escaping that way.

She glanced around the small, elegant prison. Besides the door to the hall, there was a closet and a small bathroom with a minuscule shower.

She was trapped. No one from E.D.G.E. knew where she was. She bit her lip. Did anyone from E.D.G.E. actually *care* where she was?

She sat on the bed. *No more self-pity,* she decided. It wasn't helping her.

She knew Chuck cared, but the way he'd avoided her gaze back at the office made her wonder if he doubted her too. And even if Jake had gotten her message, unless he'd seen the car she'd been forced into, he'd have no way to track her here. Wherever *here* was.

No, she was on her own. She dug her fingers into her hair. It reminded her of Vladimir's hands on her and she shuddered. What was she going to do? What if Vladimir came to her room later?

She jumped up from the bed and began pacing. She forced thoughts of Vladimir away and unbidden memories of Jake replaced them. Her heartbeat started to steady. Even the thought of him made her feel more secure. Jake represented honor and strength versus Vladimir's greed and deceit. Vladimir was no match for Jake.

She paused. *She* was no match for Jake.

He'd been so strong and yet so tender last night. They'd had a connection, she'd swear to it. But did he actually trust her? When she went missing, would he know she'd had no choice but to do this by herself?

Her shoulders slumped and she continued to pace. Now was not the time to think about Jake. If she wanted to escape, she needed to pretend to be Vladimir's *Kotyonok*. She needed her emotional armor and all her cunning, because she was back where she'd started five years ago.

On her own.

Jake placed his palms on the conference table in front of him, pushing as if he could shove his hands through the wood. "This is my fault."

Marc Koven stood on the other side of the table, his arms crossed and a muscle jumping in his jaw. "This is not your fault. We couldn't know the Rusakovs would move so fast."

"A member of my team," Jake said, though Dani was so much more than that now, "is out there without backup."

Blackwell stood at the head of the table. "Relax, Harrison. We'll find her. We have Research and IT going over every property and business belonging to the Rusakov family."

It wasn't enough. They all knew it. Without a solid lead, Dani would be dead or beyond their reach within twenty-four hours.

And she thought he didn't care. His gut churned. He wanted to punch something, or better yet, someone, but instead he pulled his hands to his sides, unable to stop them from clenching into fists.

"Dani's tough," Chuck said from his seat. His words were meant to be optimistic, but his haggard face told another story. Dani's disappearance was taking its toll on the guy. "She knows these guys," Chuck said. "She can buy some time until we find her."

But she didn't know they were looking. Rhys gripped his shoulder and Jake forced himself to nod in agreement. Now was not the time to lose it. He needed a clear head to focus.

They'd found Tassia within minutes of her escape, via the GPS tracker on all E.D.G.E. vehicles. She'd told them what Dani had done.

Jake's pride swelled at Dani's bravery. She was a rare woman, one who sacrificed her own safety for others. Her methods might not always be orthodox, but her bravery, quick thinking, and unique skillset would make her an asset to any of the E.D.G.E. teams. He wanted the chance to tell her that. And to take her out on a real date so they could continue to explore what was between them.

His head lifted. "I've got an idea."

"All ears," Koven said.

"This Vladimir is obsessed with Dani and a perfect example of an abusive boyfriend."

Chuck nodded. "True."

"Let's use that," Jake said. "The thing that a possessive boyfriend hates the most is when his girl goes out with another guy. He's already seen me with Dani at the party. So now I'll let him find me."

"Find you?" Chuck asked.

"I'll be very visible at Dani's apartment."

Koven shook his head. "I see where you're going with this, but they might just kill you, rather than take you to where they're holding Dani."

Jake crossed his arms. "It's a chance I have to take."

CHAPTER 18

D ani woke with a start, rolling off the bed and into a crouch before she'd even processed what had woken her. She still wore her clothes from yesterday and the duvet was barely wrinkled from where she'd slept on top of it. The idea of being under the covers had seemed too confining and vulnerable.

Someone rapped sharply on her door.

"What do you want?" she yelled, opening her curtains and eyeing the sun just peeking over the horizon. "It's barely morning."

The key turned in the lock and she took a few steps back, muscles tensing.

"I'm Anya," a soft voice said in Russian. "I was told to bring you breakfast." A petite blonde entered with a tray of food. She set it on the desk. Her head tilted as she studied Dani, before her lips twisted. "I will be back in thirty minutes to take you to Vladimir. Be ready." Then she disappeared, quick and quiet like a mouse—albeit a mouse who had the ability to lock the cat in a trap.

Dani sighed. She'd missed her chance to overpower Anya. Maybe when she came back. The morning sunlight shone through the window and Dani stepped into it, warmed through the glass. Fields of wheat waved in the breeze outside.

She was far out in the country from the looks of it, and she needed a plan to escape or she wouldn't stand a chance of reaching freedom. She nixed the idea of overpowering Anya until she knew more about her prison.

Orange juice, oatmeal, and a cup of coffee were her breakfast. Dani dug in, not knowing when they'd feed her again. She ate every spoonful of the bland cereal, even though she wasn't hungry. Afterward, she washed up and sat on the bed waiting for Anya's return.

Two sharp raps and the door unlocked. "It's time," Anya said in her soft voice.

Dani followed her into the hall and found Ivan and Boris waiting, their shoulder holsters visible and their eyes sharp.

"Hey, boys," Dani said. "You miss me? How's that knee, Ivan?"

Anya frowned disapprovingly at her, but didn't say anything. Dani slipped into her old bravado as if she were squeezing into a tight sweater. It didn't quite fit, but she'd make it look good before it split at the seams.

Anya led the way down the stairs and to the front door. "Vladimir is in the small red building." She pointed to one next to the barn.

Dani strode down the steps, knowing the Boulder Brothers followed her closely. She acted as if she didn't care they were there, though she had to wipe her wet palms discreetly on her jeans.

A woman's scream ripped through the air. It had come from the barn. She froze and her gut clenched. Ivan and Boris laughed and shoved her forward.

Dani refused to look back at the barn, but she vowed to figure out what was going on at this farm, and to stop it.

At the red building, Ivan knocked on the door before entering. It was basically another simple, open building, though there was an office with a large glass window looking into the main room. Two long tables covered in maps and papers stood in the center of the room, while desks with computers lined the far wall.

Two men worked at the computers, while Vladimir and another man with a sharp hooked nose stood talking by one of the center tables. Vladimir looked over as they entered.

"*Kotyonok*," he said. "Come and see where you'll be working for us."

She stood her ground. "I'm not doing anything illegal."

Vladimir held a hand against his chest in mock surprise before he laughed. "You are so predictable, Danika. You *will* do what I tell you." He jerked his head at the brothers. "Show her the barn."

Ivan and Boris grinned as they gripped her arms, frogmarching her to the barn. She didn't resist, though she really didn't want to see what was inside. The door creaked as Ivan opened it and Boris pushed her inside, still holding her arms. Moans and whimpers reached her first, and then the stink of piss, sour sweat, and burnt meat. Her brain tried to process what she was seeing.

There were no horse stalls here, just shipping crates stacked along the walls and an old panel van parked by the sliding doors on the far side. The moans came from two large cages, one on either side of the barn. Women huddled inside, most young, all of them naked. The ones in the left cage crouched, wide-eyed with fear, while the ones in the right lay listless and moaning.

In front of her, a man tended hot coals in a metal cylinder. Slender iron poles about three feet long stuck out of the embers. Her stomach started to roil. Branding irons.

Four men approached the cage on the left. All the women there moved away from the door when it swung open. The men grabbed a woman, who shrieked and flailed, desperate for escape.

Shock solidified Dani's muscles. She couldn't move while the men dragged the young woman over to the branding fire. They threw her to the ground and held her face down, each man on one of her outstretched limbs. Her face rose up toward Dani.

"*Pomogite mne!*" she screamed. "Help me! Please!"

Dani jerked as if slapped in the face. She started toward the woman, only to be hauled back into place by Boris and Ivan.

"*Nyet*," Dani screamed at the men. "Stop this. Now."

But everyone ignored her, and the brothers had learned their lesson about her feet. They avoided her kicks easily.

The man by the fire pulled one of the irons from the coals. The woman on the ground screamed as he matter-of-factly shoved it against her shoulder blade. The woman's shrieks couldn't drown out the sizzle of her flesh. The brand lifted and the man jerked his head. "Done."

The other men stood up, releasing the woman, but she didn't move. She lay sprawled on the ground, moaning and weeping. A small 'R' of blackened skin with red, raw edges showed on her pale back.

Dani looked at the other women in the cage on the right. All had a similar brand. She swallowed back bile and didn't protest when the brothers pulled her back outside. She dragged in mouthfuls of fresh air and fell to her knees.

"Get up," Ivan said. "Vladimir wants you to work now."

Dani took a last shuddering breath before standing up. She grit her teeth and walked with the two brutes back to their boss, trying to find her emotional armor again. She couldn't think about the plight of those women. She couldn't or she'd crack.

Vladimir's smirk almost made her lose it. He'd probably been watching her when she'd fallen.

"Why the brand?" she asked, keeping her voice even and trying to sound bored. "It's disgusting. Don't your clients object?"

His lips twitched as if he found her amusing. She hated him for that.

"Not at all, actually. And it's amazing what being branded does to a person," Vladimir said. "It breaks their spirit more effectively than any beating. We've had much less product loss since we've started the practice."

"Product loss?" she asked. "You mean runaways?"

He shrugged. "They can be so troublesome when they first arrive."

"Where are you finding them?" she asked.

His eyes narrowed as he studied her. "Why so curious?"

Because she wanted to get the women back to their homes. She made a decision and arched a brow. "You want me to work for you. I need to know about your business."

He didn't say anything for a moment and she wondered if she'd overplayed her hand.

"I do not trust you, *Kotyonok*," he said. "But let us see if you are worth all this trouble. Come." He waved at a workstation on the far wall. "I have a simple task for you."

She followed him to the computer and sat down at the desk. "If it's simple, then why do you need me?"

He smiled and leaned close. She wanted to pull away, but managed to stay still. "It should be simple for *you*," he said.

She placed a single finger on his chest. "We haven't discussed payment yet."

He struck like a snake, fast and vicious. He grabbed her hair in one hand and had his pistol pointed at her temple before she could do anything to stop him.

He whispered in her ear, "Your payment is your life."

Her heart hammered and she froze, afraid to make any sudden moves. She swallowed. She needed to prove to Vladimir that she wasn't a victim or she'd lose his interest and find herself branded, drugged, and on sale before she could set her fingers to the keyboard.

She exhaled slowly and raised her hand from where it was splayed on his chest to the pistol. She used one finger again, but this time ever so slowly, she touched the barrel of the pistol and gently pushed it away from her temple. "I see your point," she said evenly. "What would you like me to do?"

He let her move the gun aside. At the same time, he stood up, towering over her. He hadn't released his grip on her hair and he tilted her face so he could see it. Rage curled inside her gut and she wanted to rip away from him. But she lifted her chin even higher, letting nothing of her hatred show in her eyes.

His smile came slowly. "I want you to hack into U.S. Customs and Border Protection."

Dani had just finished the dinner Anya had brought her when the door unlocked and Vladimir strolled in. The Boulder Brothers waited in the hall.

She stood up but didn't back away, even though she wanted to. "What do you want?"

"*Kotyonok*," he said, drawing the hated nickname out. "I came to visit my old friend. We are friends, are we not?"

She crossed her arms over her chest. "Friends don't hold guns to your head."

He sat down on her bed and smiled. "I wanted your attention, and for you to realize how serious this is."

"Fine," Dani said. "I'm working for you and, believe me, I know it's serious."

His hand smoothed over the duvet cover, back and forth, as if caressing it, his dark eyes focused on her. "Won't you join me?"

"What do you want, Vladimir? I'm tired."

"Ah, I see," he said. "You're going to play hard to get. I understand. It is your right as a woman to dictate how fast the relationship goes."

She froze, his words like tiny grenades waiting to explode if she touched them wrong. "We don't have a relationship. We haven't for a long time."

He stood and stalked over to her. His hand swept her hair back behind her ear and then trailed down her neck. She shuddered in revulsion, but didn't move otherwise. "You remember how good we were together," he whispered. "You just won't admit it."

She shook her head and he put a finger to her lips. "I will give you time to get used to me again," he said. His smile scared her more than the threat of branding. "But not too much. I find I'm impatient to have you."

He walked to the door and rapped once. Ivan unlocked it and pushed it open.

"Dream of me, *Kotyonok*," Vladimir said before locking her back in.

Dani sagged onto the bed.

The next day, Dani felt like a tightrope walker as she sat at her workstation, her fingers typing slowly as she dragged her way through the assigned hack.

She struggled to keep up her tough persona, proving to Vladimir she was trustworthy, and yet holding back enough so as to not provoke him to violence.

All day she'd attempted to hack her way into the Customs and Border Protection network. It was slow, delicate work. She wasn't part of the hacktivist group Anonymous, or any kind of super hacker. She was out of practice for this type of job, but she knew she'd eventually do it and the thought of helping Vladimir made her gut churn.

He wanted the trucks carrying his cargo of trafficked women to be passed right through customs without inspection. Once in their network, it would be easy to give the green light to the trucks. Apparently, Vladimir had buyers all over the States, but he lost too much of his profits getting around the CBP.

She didn't want Vladimir's trucks to be passed over for inspection. So she kept making minor mistakes in her programs, little bugs that she had to fix. If she kept going the way she was, she'd be caught by CBP.

She stopped typing, an idea forming. If she could lead the CBP to her, then maybe they would storm this place. She'd probably end up in prison, but at least she'd stop Vladimir and his sick business.

And prison might be safer than here.

With a set jaw, she started to lay the groundwork, the trail of breadcrumbs that would bring CBP to her. She had to be careful; Vladimir had another tech geek checking on her while she worked. He was Vladimir's cousin, about her age and straight from Moscow. His English sucked, though his computer skills weren't horrible.

A real smile tugged at her lips. But she was better.

That night, Vladimir had dinner in her room. The Boulder Brothers brought in a small table, while Anya set it with elegant tableware. Dinner consisted of prime rib au jus, roasted potatoes, and braised carrots. The red wine was dry and full-bodied. The candlelight washed their faces in a warm glow.

She wished foolishly that Jake sat across from her.

"*Kotyonok*, you've barely touched your food. Is it not to your liking?"

It tasted like ashes in her mouth. "It's fine. I guess I'm just not that hungry."

"Come now, are you sulking? Where is my fiery *Kotyonok*?"

She lowered her eyes so he wouldn't see the hate she couldn't hide when he referenced their time together. She made herself start eating, if only to keep her strength up, though she passed over the wine for a glass of water.

Vladimir spoke of trivial things like movies and celebrity gossip. Dani chatted back, and if her tone wasn't as carefree, he didn't seem to notice. At least her smile was genuine, as she kept picturing shoving her fork into his eye.

After dinner, Vladimir ran a hand down her arm. "We need to get you some proper clothes, Danika. I dislike seeing you in jeans and t-shirts. You dress like a boy."

Dani grit her teeth. "New clothes might be nice. But I'm not your harlot."

He smiled. "Of course not, *Kotyonok*." The hand trailing along her arm came up to cup her face. He leaned down and kissed her, gentle and slow. His lips reminded her of warm slugs, squishy and a bit wet.

Instead of stabbing him like she wanted, she gently pushed him away. "It's too soon."

His eyes narrowed, and she kept her revulsion buried deep, only showing him a blank face. Finally he nodded. "Goodnight, Danika."

Alone, she scrubbed at her mouth. She wasn't going to be able to wait for CBP to be her rescue. She had to escape soon, before Vladimir decided to force their relationship to the next level.

CHAPTER 19

The next day, Dani shoved back from the workstation. "I need a break."

Vladimir was no longer in the room, but two men worked at the other stations and the Boulder Brothers stood by the door.

"*Nyet*. No breaks," Ivan said.

"I worked through lunch. I'm hungry."

He smirked. "You can eat later."

"*Mudak*," she said, calling him an asshole. "I'm going to the bathroom."

"Make it quick."

She gave him the finger as she walked to the door beside the glass-walled office. In the bathroom, she took care of her needs and then splashed water on her face. She eyed the mirror. She could break it and hold a piece of the glass wrapped in her shirt, but the brothers would hear the mirror break and be waiting for her with guns drawn. She didn't fancy dying in just her bra.

She snorted at herself. Did it really matter what she was wearing if she was dead? The stress of the situation was obviously getting to her.

She stepped out of the washroom to find Vladimir waiting for her with a childish look of glee on his face. Nausea swirled inside her. Whatever had put that look there couldn't possibly be good for her.

"There you are, *Kotyonok*," he said. "What news do you have for me?"

She crossed her arms. "It's slow work. There's a ton of security on the site. It'll take at least a week to hack it." And she planned to be long gone by then. Somehow.

He shook his head. "That won't do. Come. I have a present for you."

"A present?" That wasn't what she'd expected.

If anything, his excitement rose with her question and he looked as if he wanted to rub his hands together. "You could call it an incentive." He chuckled and even the Boulder Brothers cracked smiles.

He led her outside to the outbuilding he'd shown her when she'd first arrived. The one where he'd planned to punish her. Her steps slowed. Was this his present? A little mid-afternoon torture?

He turned to look back at her, the maniacal gleam in

his eye almost as disturbing as watching the woman in the barn being branded. How could she ever have let this man into her life and her bed?

"Don't be nervous, Danika. This won't hurt...*you*."

Dani didn't want to see what was behind the door, but she had no choice. Boris pushed her into the building. She didn't see anything at first as her eyes adjusted to the dim interior. The smack of flesh on flesh and a low, masculine groan jolted through her system like electricity. Her eyes widened.

Jake sat tied to the chair, wearing only a ripped black t-shirt and jeans. His feet were bare and his head lowered.

"Jake," she whispered.

His head lifted and she gasped. Blood ran from a cut over his eye, making him seem like a horror-film victim. Raw scrapes marked the other side of his face. They must have been beating him for a while.

She tried to run to him, but the brothers caught her arms and held her back.

"How?" She looked from Jake to Vladimir, who nodded at her.

"Your boyfriend is not as tough as he looks, Danika. My men subdued him easily." He shrugged. "It matters not. We have him. If you don't do what I ask then I will hurt him. If you still don't do it, I will kill him. Very simple."

She wanted to tell him that Jake wasn't her boyfriend. He wasn't her anything. But while Jake may not have strong feelings for her, she realized she had feelings for him.

Panic and pain at the sight of him tied up seared through her, making her brain numb. She couldn't let them hurt him worse than they already had. But she also knew that the safest thing for Jake was to distance him from her.

She shook off the restraining hands. "He's not my boyfriend," she said coldly.

Vladimir laughed. "You're not a very good liar, Danika. We found him at your apartment." His voice carried an edge. "Sleeping in your bed."

Vladimir no longer called her Kitten. "I'm not lying," she said. "He's someone I just met. And I have no idea what he was doing at my apartment."

"It bothers you to see him like this," Vladimir said accusingly.

She huffed, "Of course it does. I feel responsible that he's in this situation. He wouldn't be here if not for me. It's what any sane person would feel."

Vladimir scowled. "You slept with him."

"No," she said, her face flushing. "I—"

"I saw you kissing at the party," Vladimir said.

The room became quiet. Dani wanted to sigh with relief. He didn't know about what had happened at the hotel. For a minute she'd been sure Vladimir had found a way to spy on her.

"She's a tease." Jake's voice rasped like stinging wasps. "Little bitch led me on."

Dani's horrified gasp echoed in the room. Vladimir turned to face Jake. "What did you say?"

"I *said*, the bitch led me on." Jake's jaw jutted out. "It's why I was at her place. She owed me after I rented that tux for the fancy party she wanted to go to."

Dani felt off-balance as Jake's hard gaze scanned her curves. "Feeling her tits wasn't worth this kind of trouble."

Vladimir's eyes narrowed as he studied first Jake and then Dani, before swiveling to fully face Jake. "You're either very stupid or very brave." He snorted. "I'm thinking stupid. But let's just have a little test, shall we?"

He crooked a finger at Boris, who lumbered over. Vladimir nodded at Jake and then focused his attention on Dani. She knew what was coming and steeled herself. She had no idea why Jake was provoking Vladimir, but she wouldn't add to his torment by showing that she cared.

Boris made a fist and struck Jake in the gut. Hard. Jake exhaled heavily and gave a small groan. He hit him twice more and each time, Jake slumped farther in his chair.

Boris straightened and looked to Vladimir. At that exact moment, Jake raised his head and winked at her, before letting his head loll forward again.

Dani froze. What the hell? Was he trying to be brave? To reassure her? Did he not realize he was tied to a chair and being tortured?

Dani fought to keep any emotion off her face as Boris punched Jake twice more.

"Enough," she said. She didn't know what Jake was doing, but she hated standing there and watching him get hurt. Vladimir raised a hand and Boris stepped back from

Jake.

"Seriously, Vladimir?" she said. "Do I really need to watch this? I'm already working for you."

Vladimir chewed his lip a moment. "Perhaps you're right. This probably isn't the best use of your time, *Kotyonok*." He waved a hand at Jake. "I will deal with this *mudak* while you get back to work."

Her stomach dropped, but she swallowed and asked calmly, "Are you going to kill him?"

He looked at her slyly. "Not until we find your friend Tassia. Until then, we'll use him to keep you from escaping. You may not care for him, but I do believe you've become softhearted enough to not want his death on your hands." He smirked. "I will see you tonight, *Kotyonok*."

Jake's head snapped up and his gaze seared her. She ignored it, gritted her teeth, and smiled at Vladimir. It was part of the plan, she chanted to herself.

But as Ivan escorted her back across the field, the hurt and rage she'd seen in Jake's eyes haunted her.

When the sun set that day, the Boulder Brothers escorted her back to the main farmhouse. Anya brought her a simple dinner of bread and stew, and locked the door behind her, leaving Dani alone in the room with her thoughts.

Vladimir clearly wasn't joining her for dinner and a sigh of relief escaped her. She ate quickly and then started to pace.

How had Vladimir managed to capture Jake? He was a freaking Navy SEAL. Wasn't he supposed to be superhuman or something? How had Vladimir's less-than-capable thugs overcome Jake?

Her head snapped up. They hadn't. They couldn't overcome a SEAL. She'd fought Vladimir's men herself, and had almost overpowered them.

No, they didn't capture Jake. He'd let himself be taken. He'd done it to help her. That thought stunned her for a moment. She sank onto the bed. He'd been trying to help her.

But what had his plan been? Why had he let himself be tied up? Maybe they'd drugged him like they had her. She needed to get to him and untie him. Then he could help her rescue the women in the cages.

First, she had to get out of this room.

She pounded on her door, hoping Anya would come back. She jumped back when only a few seconds later someone unlocked it. The door pushed open and Dani forced herself to smile, though it was the last person she wanted to see.

Vladimir walked into the room with a bottle of wine and two glasses, and Boris closed the door behind him.

"Impatient?" he murmured.

"I'm tired of being locked up all the time. Can't we go for a walk?" She made her lips pout just a little. *Or maybe I could just kick you in the balls*, she thought. But she needed him to get the door open first so she could escape.

"Maybe later," he said, his gaze crawling over her. "If you're good."

She swallowed the bile that rose and continued to smile, before she unzipped her hoodie and tossed it onto the desk chair, leaving her only in a black tank top and jeans. Tonight she played a dangerous game.

"Are you going to pour me a glass?" she asked, sitting on the foot of the bed. She leaned back on her palms, knowing it did good things for her small chest. "It's been a long day."

Vladimir focused on the swell of her breasts before setting the glasses on the desk and pouring red wine into them. "I'm happy to see that you're being reasonable."

She needed to tread carefully. If she acquiesced too easily then he'd know something was up. Vladimir wasn't stupid. "Let's get this straight," Dani said. "I'm not happy about being locked up and given no choice in the work I do."

He studied her like she was a chessboard. "But?"

She shrugged. "But if you're ever going to let me go, then I need to start proving my loyalty."

His head tilted, while his eyes zeroed in on hers. "You're loyal to me?"

She held his gaze and stood up, walking toward him. "I was loyal to you and the Rusakov family once. I can be loyal again." She reached around him and took one of the wine glasses and sipped. "For the right price."

His shoulders relaxed and he smiled. "And there it is. What price are you looking for, Danika?" His smile sharpened to a blade's edge. "Remember, you're not exactly in a position to bargain."

"I want my freedom," she said. She let a smile grow on her lips. "Okay, and maybe a small paycheck wouldn't be frowned upon."

Her stomach tightened when he didn't answer right away. Had she pushed too much? His gaze held hers and she cocked an eyebrow as she waited, the portrait of confidence, though her palms were slick with sweat.

Vladimir grinned. "It's good to have you back, *Kotyonok*. I will speak with my father about bringing you on payroll."

"What about getting me out of this room?"

He took her wine and set the glass down on the desk. "I find I like having you right where I can find you."

She gritted her teeth. "It's pretty easy to find me at my apartment."

He moved closer to her. "I think I will keep you caged near me for a few more days, until I'm satisfied with your... loyalty."

She hadn't realized she'd been backing up, until she felt the bed hit her calves. She swallowed. He stood only inches away from her, and his hot breath touched her cheek. She had to stop this now.

"Just because I'm working for you as a hacker doesn't mean I'm going to fall back into bed with you," she said.

"It was good between us," Vladimir said. "Don't you miss it?"

"No," she said.

"Liar."

She almost laughed. Vladimir's ego was the key to her escape. She just needed to figure out how to use it.

He leaned in and kissed her. She pulled back automatically and his arms came around her like steel bands, trapping her against him. She started to struggle and his hand dug into her hair, gripping the back of her head, guiding her so he could slant his mouth over hers.

She should play along with the kiss, but she couldn't. Not again. She knew that this time he wouldn't stop with a kiss.

Something inside her screamed to get away. His hands tightened further as if he knew she was going to resist. His tongue pushed against her lips.

No. No. No, rang through her mind.

"Stop fighting me, *Kotyonok*." His voice was ragged and she could feel his erection against her stomach. He nuzzled her neck and she shivered in dread. "You want me," he said.

She knew what she had to do. She hoped she had the stomach for it.

Dani forced herself to relax in his arms, her shoulders slumping as she leaned toward him. She let her head fall back, giving him greater access to her neck. He growled approvingly, taking her shudders to be desire and not revulsion.

She would only have one chance. When next he kissed her, she opened her mouth and let him in. His tongue thrust against hers. His hands still gripped her upper arms, holding her tightly. She needed her arms free, so she put her hands on his chest and spread her fingers, digging her nails in through his shirt. "Let me touch you," she gasped.

His hands slid from her arms to her back, sweeping up and down. One slid around to her front, squeezing her breasts, and she let out a small groan, hating what she was doing and hating Vladimir for making her.

She slid her hands behind his neck, digging them into his hair. She needed to act fast before he could shout for help.

She kissed him, openmouthed, and let his tongue back into her mouth. She gripped his hair tight.

And then, she bit down. She held Vladimir's tongue between her teeth. At the same time, she kneed him between his legs. He yelled into her mouth and his one hand wrenched at her hair, pulling painfully on her scalp.

She let his tongue go, but yanked his head down to meet her rising knee. It connected with his face. His hand loosened on her hair as he grunted. She did it again and again.

He slid to the floor, unconscious, and she let him. She spat his blood from her mouth. Time to tie the psycho up.

Within minutes, using his shoelaces, she had his hands tied behind his back. She shoved one of her socks from her pack into his mouth. It wouldn't hold him forever, but any extra time she could get she'd take.

She searched him thoroughly, but he had no key, no weapons, and no cell. Useless tool. She wanted to kick him again, but didn't have time. He'd wake soon and start making noise. Time to deal with the Boulder Brothers. She looked at the door and sucked in a breath.

The door handle turned slowly and silently. Had the brothers heard something? Her heart stuttered and she jumped for the corked wine bottle on the desk. She held it like a weapon and stood beside the door, ready to strike.

CHAPTER 20

Jake slumped when the overweight muscleman escorted Dani from the room. He hated this deception, but kept going with it. Groaning, he pretended to pass out after another couple of punches.

He'd had worse on SERE—the Survival, Evasion, Resistance, and Escape course that all spec ops had to go through. The SERE instructors who taught resistance to interrogation had prepared him for situations like this.

Jake would be covered in bruises tomorrow, but he knew how to tighten his muscles before a hit so the guy couldn't crack a rib.

Hopefully.

Besides, a few bruises were worth it, if it gave him a chance to get Dani out of here.

And he would get her out.

He listened while Vladimir made jokes in both Russian and English about Jake and how he would die later. Jake assumed Vladimir tested him to see if he spoke Russian or if he was awake. His threats were laughable. He stayed slumped. The door opened and closed with a click.

He waited, calm and unmoving, counting his heartbeats. He reached seventy-eight before Vladimir spoke again.

"Next time, do not hit him so hard, Boris. We won't learn anything if you kill him too soon."

The door opened and shut again, but this time their conversation and footsteps signaled that they'd actually left the building.

Jake sat up. Time to free himself and get Dani out of here. He hadn't liked the sound of Vladimir's parting comment to her. Had the asshole been forcing himself on her?

He ground his teeth while he worked the bonds securing his wrists to the chair. It was simple, slender rope and Jake pulled on one wrist hard so the rope tightened around the other. He tugged so much that it cut off circulation in his left hand, and yet he kept pulling and twisting, trying to give his right hand room to move.

In only a few minutes he had his right hand free. One more and he'd undone the rope securing his left hand to the chair. He stood and his leg almost gave out on him. It quivered and tightened, threatening to cramp.

He rubbed it hard, pushing against the muscles and scar tissue, trying to make it relax. He didn't have time for this.

But he forced himself to breathe evenly and take care of his leg. A minute now would save him writhing in pain later. The muscles loosened and he eased his ministrations, moving to the window near the door.

Thankfully, the sun was setting. When full dark fell, his team would come in. For now, they'd be waiting out there somewhere.

It had been Jake's idea to wait at Dani's apartment in the hopes that the Rusakov family would grab him, thinking he might be useful as leverage against Dani. SEALs never surrendered, but if Dani could give herself up to save someone, then he could let himself be taken as a ploy to find her.

Unfortunately, he couldn't wear a wire or bring a weapon, but that hadn't really deterred him. He knew Rhys was more than capable of following them undetected. Blackwell's other team members seemed reasonably competent, as well.

It had taken two damn days of waiting around for the Rusakovs to show up. Two damn days of worrying and pacing.

Jake had put up very little fight when they'd shown up, so impatient was he to find out where they'd been holding Dani. The farm was a surprise. It hadn't been on any of E.D.G.E.'s lists of suspected properties.

He should wait until full dark before going after Dani, but his unease grew at the thought of her alone, facing off against Vladimir. Logically, he knew she could take care of herself. He'd seen her fight at the gym and she wasn't someone who gave up, but the thought of Vladimir running his hands over her made Jake's gut burn. He would kill the man if he touched Dani.

Jake kept watch out the window, trying unsuccessfully to control his emotions. Always before on missions, he'd been able to clear his mind for the task at hand. He couldn't seem to do that with Dani. She kept forcing her way into his thoughts. He didn't know what that said about him.

A lot of activity around the barn caught his eye and quieted his mind. Men opened up the large barn doors and stood watching the road leading to the farm. Jake eyed the road too, and soon a dust trail could be seen. A large truck drove up the road and slowly rumbled to a stop inside the barn. The men shut the doors behind it.

It looked like another shipment had just come in. If it was women, like he suspected, then he knew he wouldn't be going anywhere until he'd freed them.

But first he had to free Dani.

He cursed softly when he saw two men walking toward his building. He briefly debated his choices, before moving back to the chair and placing his hands behind his back as if tied up. He let his head slump forward and closed his eyes.

A moment later, the door opened and the two men entered speaking in Russian.

"What does Vladimir want us to do with him?" one asked.

"Hurt him a bit. Make him wish he'd never laid eyes on that *blya*."

Jake's teeth clenched when they called Dani a whore.

"Wake up, *mudak*," one of them said.

Jake didn't move. He needed them to come a bit closer.

"Ivan was right," the other said. "For all his muscles, this guy's a pussy."

Come closer, Jake thought. He cracked his eyes open the barest fraction of an inch. A pair of Adidas sneakers stood right by his chair, the man turned to his friend.

Close enough.

Jake sprang at him, sending a vicious uppercut with all of his body weight behind it into the man's chin. He sagged and Jake leapt at the other man, who started to draw his gun from a shoulder holster. Jake gave a hard right cross to his cheek, stunning him. Then he grabbed his gun arm and twisted, while sweeping one foot behind the other man's and pushing him off-balance. He fell and Jake followed him down, planting a hard elbow strike across the guy's temple. His head bounced once on the concrete floor and his body went lax.

Jake grabbed the man's gun and spun to face his partner. He shouldn't have worried. That one was still sprawled by the chair. Jake nodded in satisfaction and contemplated killing them, but decided against it. Instead, he used the rope and tied them up. They wouldn't get loose from his knots so easily.

When he looked back out the window, darkness

shrouded the field, though lights from the barn and main house gave off enough glow to see anyone walking. He would prefer complete darkness to work in, but he'd make do.

He stripped the gun and shoulder holster from the other man and put them on. Conscious of his bare feet, he eyed the men's shoes, but neither of them had feet near his size. He shrugged and left the room, one gun in hand and the other holstered, both with full magazines.

He walked with determined strides to the house. If anyone looked outside, he hoped they'd just see another guard walking, and not a barefoot escaped prisoner. He bypassed the back door of the house and stalked along the side, studying the second floor.

There.

A window open to the evening breeze.

Jake contemplated killing the dickhead who'd cracked his rib, but instead loosened the chokehold at the last second so the man's unconscious form slid to the hallway floor. The key to the bedroom door was on a chain around the guy's neck.

Jake suspected Dani was inside, but didn't know if she was alone. He couldn't hear anything as he turned the doorknob soundlessly and cracked the door open the barest inch.

His instincts warned him someone waited for him

inside. He thrust open the door, ducked down and into the room, gun out, scanning for targets.

Someone swung at him. He grabbed the person's arm and twisted until they dropped the weapon. The curse told him who it was. A wine bottle rolled away and he pulled Dani into his arms, her back to his chest, tightening his grip when she continued to struggle.

She cursed him again and he almost laughed.

"Relax, hacker girl. It's me," Jake said in her ear.

She whirled in his arms and hugged him tight. He winced as she pressed down on his bruised ribs. She loosened her grip, but he tightened his arms around her before she could pull away. She snuggled into him and he pressed his lips to the top of her head, enjoying having her safe in his arms. "I've got you."

She mumbled something into his chest.

"What's that?" he asked.

She lifted her head. "I didn't think you'd come for me."

He cupped her face in his hands. "I'll always come for you."

Her eyes widened and her lips parted. He leaned down and pressed his mouth to hers. They didn't have time, but he had to touch her, claim her, if only for a moment. His hands slid down her back, molding her to him. He demanded she melt for him, and she did.

When he lifted his head, her hands clutched his t-shirt and he grinned, the awful feeling of losing her fading with her nearness. He lifted her hands from his shirt and squeezed them. "We'll finish this when we get out of here."

Dani's face turned red and she ducked her head. He let her go. Time to get back in the game. He checked the hallway before dragging Dickhead's body into the room and shutting the door.

"How'd you get here?" she asked him. "You were tied up. I was coming to rescue you."

Jake looked beyond her, at Vladimir's limp form, and scowled. "And I came to rescue *you*."

She flipped her hair over her shoulder and grinned. "I can take care of myself."

Something didn't ring true with that statement. "Are you okay?" he asked. She seemed to be moving well. "Did he hurt you?"

A shadow crossed her eyes, and he wanted to pound the shit out of the guy, even if he *was* unconscious.

"I'm good," she said. "Besides, I won."

The anger in him slowly banked and his lips twitched. "I noticed."

"Should we tie him up?" Dani asked, pointing at Dickhead.

"He's not going to wake up for a while," Jake said, moving to the window to shift aside the curtain slightly. The team should have been here by now. Something must have happened. For now, they were on their own. "Besides, we need to get you out of here."

She pulled on her pack. "What do you mean, get me out of here?"

"The team isn't here," he said. "But if you stay in the shadows and follow the road out, you should run into help eventually."

"What about you?"

"I still have work to do."

She straightened and got that stubborn look in her eye. "Like rescue the women in the barn?"

"You've seen them?"

She glared at him now. "I am not leaving without them."

He frowned. How could he make sure she was safe and still complete the mission?

She sighed. "I'm not like your college girlfriend, Jake. You don't have to protect me." Dani swept an arm toward the downed men. "I can take care of myself."

He studied her without speaking. She was right. She was as different from his old girlfriend as he was from the college boy who hadn't been able to protect her. Dani was brave and could fight, he conceded to himself.

"I have skills that you can use," she said, as if she'd heard his inner thoughts. "It doesn't make sense to send me away."

He stayed silent, assessing her words. She did have skills. He'd seen them.

Her intense blue eyes held him in thrall. "I may not have military training," she said, "but you know I can do this job."

She was tough, brave, and smart. She was right. She could do this job, and it was up to him to deal with any distractions she posed for him. Besides, it'd be good to have someone watching his back. The tension left him and he nodded. "Let's rock and roll."

Her eyes widened as if she hadn't expected him to agree. He almost laughed. She argued like a lawyer and then was surprised when she won.

She exhaled slowly. "You won't regret it."

"I know," he said, moving into the hallway, all business again. "Now, let's move."

CHAPTER 21

Dani gripped the drainpipe beside the second-floor window and swung out onto it. Jake already crouched on the ground in the shadows, his gun out, scanning the darkness. She could see that he put more weight on his good leg, but she thought that might almost be an unconscious move, habit rather than necessity.

They'd escaped the main house the same way Jake had gotten in. He'd made the descent look easy. It wasn't. She had to use all her upper body strength as well as her legs, but she was used to climbing the ropes at her gym. This wasn't too different. Except for the fact that there were no mats to cushion her if she fell.

She shimmied to the ground and hopped off to land

soundlessly beside Jake.

She tapped his shoulder, the agreed-upon signal, and he took off to the barn with her running in a crouch behind him. Jake hadn't offered to help her at all. He'd just assumed she'd scale the pipe. She thought she loved him a little for that.

She stumbled at the unexpected thought.

Jake's head whipped around. She waved at him that she was okay and they kept going. They made it to the barn and ducked into the deep shadows beside it.

Love? No, she thought. She couldn't love him. Not yet.

The thought almost tripped her up again. Was she even ready to love? Could she open her heart and soul to Jake? She watched his tall form move with predatory grace, sliding through the darkness, not missing a detail. He was a warrior first and foremost, but he was also a man. Someone warm, funny, and compassionate.

She bit her lip. Now was not the time to be thinking of this. She had to get her head in the game, as Jake would say, or someone might blow it off. That thought chilled her and she concentrated on not being seen.

They came upon a filthy window. Jake glanced through it while she kept watch.

He swore softly. "They're in cages."

"I know," she said.

He moved away from the window and close to her. "Four men. Lucky for us they're all sitting together at a table in the middle of the room playing cards."

They crept to the corner of the barn, then Jake stopped and pulled the gun from his shoulder holster and handed it to her, handle first.

"I'm not good with a gun," she whispered.

"Safety's off. Don't put your finger on the trigger until you mean to shoot. Use two hands," he said, demonstrating. "One to hold and one to steady. Aim for the chest. Pull the trigger. Simple."

She swallowed. The women inside the barn needed her help and so did Jake, whether he knew it or not. She took the gun and nodded. "Got it. Point and shoot."

He winked. "You'll be fine. Leave the shooting to me. Only fire if fired upon."

He crept to the corner of the barn and peeked around. He motioned her forward. "I'm going in first. I'll clear the guards. Give me thirty seconds and then come in."

She nodded and gripped the gun in two hands. Jake took her hands and pulled her index finger off the trigger and laid it alongside the barrel of the gun. Then he leaned in and gave her a short, hard kiss before dashing around the corner, leaving her breathless.

While she counted she heard the crack of two gunshots, some shouting, and a few more shots. It was noisier than she'd expected. At thirty, she went around the corner to the door. No one approached from the outside and she opened the door and leapt inside, gun up.

Jake stood by himself in the middle of the room. "It's good, Dani," he said, walking past the bodies of the four guards. "Gun down."

She panted a little, but nodded and lowered her weapon. About ten women waited, tense and frozen in the cage on the right. A large padlock held the door closed. "Pick the lock or hotwire the car?" she asked.

"Lady's choice," he said with a grin.

"The guards probably have a key." She looked again at the bodies of the men, blood spreading in pools around them. She had no desire to search them. "I'll hotwire." She jogged over to the panel van parked beside the moving truck.

Jake searched the bodies for a key while she clambered into the van, setting her gun down on the seat beside her. Thankfully, it was an older model from the nineties. She pulled her pack off and dug into it until she found her makeup case and her nail clippers.

She pried the plastic cover off the steering column to find the bundle of wires for the battery, ignition, and starter. The battery wires were red and easy to separate from the others. She used her clippers to strip off a bit of the insulating rubber from each one, as well as from the brown ignition wire. Then she wove them together.

The van's dash lights and radio came on. She clicked off the music and listened. She thought she heard a shout, but didn't hear anything more. Probably one of the women Jake was freeing. She continued with her work and pulled out the yellow starter wire and stripped it. All she had to do now was spark it against the woven battery and ignition wires and the truck should start. She left it hanging, careful that it didn't touch any metal, but ready to use.

She sat back up to check Jake's progress. A gasp left her when Ivan stepped up to the open truck door, holding a gun aimed at her head. "Stupid *blya*. Mr. Rusakov is pissed." He waved at her to get out. "You and your boyfriend will pay."

Jake shouted something on the other side of the barn.

She lifted her hands as she stepped out of the truck. "Take it easy, Ivan."

"Move it," he said. "The boss wants you."

Gunshots rang out and Ivan turned his head to the back of the barn. Dani ducked and punched him hard in the groin. He bent over, growling and swinging the gun toward her. She swept his gun arm aside with her forearm. It fired twice into the truck behind her, while she used a palm strike against his nose, following up with a vicious hit to his throat, before grabbing his hair and slamming his face against her knee.

Ivan thudded to the ground, no longer a problem. She grabbed his gun and hers before running toward the back of the barn.

With a gun in each hand, she probably looked like some kind of video-game heroine, albeit a small-chested one. She snorted. She was definitely losing it.

Jake and the women were crouched behind the moving crates stacked on the other side of the barn, while Vladimir's men arranged themselves near the backdoor. She ducked behind a crate herself and assessed the situation.

"I just want Danika," Vladimir yelled from near the

door. "I don't care about your boy toy, *Kotyonok*. He's free to go if you give yourself up to me."

She met Jake's eyes from across the barn. He shook his head at her in between firing. He must have taken the guards' guns, because he had spares beside him on the ground.

She showed him the two guns she had. "Trust me," she mouthed at him. His lips compressed and he fired once more. One of Vladimir's thugs screamed and fell. Jake looked at her a long moment and then nodded. He grabbed his spare guns and started to hustle the women to the van.

She peeked over the crate she hid behind. Two of Vladimir's men crept toward her. She set one gun aside and used two hands to steady the other. She aimed, and wondered if she should try to warn the men off before firing.

Then she remembered the branding.

She pulled the trigger.

Jake kept up a steady stream of curses in his head as he led the terrified women back to the panel van. He threw open the back doors and gestured for the women to get in. They only looked at him with frightened eyes, unable to understand his English.

"Get in," he said again. He waved his arm and looked back to the firefight he'd left Dani in. More curses boiled on his tongue, but he compressed his lips. Using Russian and a calm voice, he said, "*Spaseeba*. Please, get in. I'll take you to safety."

An older woman, maybe late thirties, nodded at him and started speaking what he thought was Ukrainian to the other women. They leapt into the van after that. Jake slammed the doors and ran to the driver's side. A fierce pride surged through him when he saw the unconscious thug and the hanging starter wire for the van. His woman had serious skills.

He checked the back of the barn, but couldn't see Dani. The gunfire hadn't lessened. Where the hell was she? Trust in her skills or not, he couldn't leave her. He wouldn't leave Rhys, so he sure as fuck was not leaving Dani behind.

He leaned into the van and spoke in Russian to the older woman. "Can you drive?"

"*Da.*"

He flicked the starter wire against the others Dani had twisted together, until it sparked and the engine turned over. He jumped out while the woman slid into the driver's seat. She yelled something back to the other women and revved the engine.

"Stop them!"

He heard the shout from behind and raced to the sliding barn doors, throwing his weight behind one and pushing it open. The woman waved at him to come back.

Jake shook his head and waved them on. The woman nodded and gunned it, screeching out of the barn and down the dark road to freedom.

He crouched by a crate and used his stolen weapons to pick off Vladimir's men as they ran toward the open barn door. His gut urged him to find Dani and get the hell out of this clusterfuck.

They'd have to play a little 'Escape and Evasion' through farmers' fields, but he was confident they could get away, if only they could get out of this barn. He began to make his way back to where he'd last seen Dani.

When he finally saw her, his heart almost gave out.

Out of the corner of her eye, Dani watched Jake herd the women toward the waiting van. She needed to get back there ASAP.

Another of Vladimir's men left cover with his gun pointed right at her. Her gut clenched and she threw herself backward. Splinters flew from the crate where her head had been.

"Don't kill her," Vladimir shouted. "I want her alive."

A frisson of fear lanced through her at his words. She pushed it aside and adjusted her grip on the gun. She panted. Vladimir's men would surround her soon. She needed to get up, but the thought of poking her head over the dubious protection of the crates paralyzed her.

She swallowed. Okay, next time, she would volunteer to hack the bad guys' systems, but no more superhero antics for her—she'd leave that to Jake. She'd had no concept before this of what his job really entailed, and now that she did, her feelings for him expanded. He'd come here alone to rescue her. He really was a hero.

She'd better not make his job any harder.

With that decision, she jumped around the far side of the crate and shot once at each of the three men heading in her direction. One of them yelped when she hit his arm, and the others ducked for cover. She crouched back down, panting. *Merde*, hitting a moving target was hard.

She didn't know how to check how many bullets were left in her gun and was afraid that even if she could get the magazine out, she wouldn't be able to put it back in. She had another gun.

She jumped up and fired once without even aiming at anything and then cursed herself for wasting a bullet. At least the thugs had hunkered down again.

She did the same, feeling a bit like one of those pop-up ducks at a kid's carnival shooting game. Hopefully, no one would win a prize. She almost giggled and knew stress was making her lose it. She had to gain control.

She popped up, fired twice, and managed to hit one man in the leg. The second time she pulled the trigger, her gun clicked ominously in the sudden quiet of the barn.

She dropped down and snatched up the next gun before leaping up again. Sure enough, Vladimir's men ran toward her position, thinking she was an easy target.

Point. Aim. Shoot.

One man clutched his chest, falling to the ground, but she moved on. The other two dove to the side.

She stayed standing, watching the fallen man struggle to breathe. Dragging her eyes away, she looked for her next target.

"Enough!" Vladimir stood up by the back barn door. "Danika, my *Kotyonok*, let us talk reasonably," Vladimir called out.

Point. She kept her arms steady and swung her weapon in his direction.

Aim. His chest was broad, but didn't seem like a big enough target, especially since he now walked slowly toward her with his hands in the air.

Shoot. Her finger tightened on the trigger.

"I'm unarmed, Danika," Vladimir called out. "You would murder a man in cold blood?"

Her breathing hitched and her finger froze on the trigger.

The sound of an engine roaring to life behind her almost startled her into pulling the trigger.

Vladimir looked beyond her, his scowl fierce. "Stop them!"

Shots rang out and some of Vladimir's men raced after the van, but Dani kept her weapon trained on Vladimir. She took a step back. The van's engine revved again. She'd better get back there now. About to drop her weapon and run, instead she froze when the van's tires squealed as it tore out of the barn and away from her.

Jake had left her.

Vladimir's enraged scowl focused on her and whatever he saw in her face made him throw his head back and laugh. "You should see your face, Danika," he said. "Why are you so shocked that no one wants you?"

She trembled with the need to pull the trigger.

His laughter died and a coldness settled over him. "It's over, Danika. Drop the gun."

She shook her head. "No freaking way."

He stopped about twenty feet from her, his hands by his sides as he glanced at her weapon. "Your arms are shaking. You've held that gun a long time now. Heavy, isn't it?"

She narrowed her eyes. She could hit him from here.

"You need to learn when to quit. Your friend, if you can call him that, left you here to die." He sighed, his voice compassionate. "I won't kill you, *Kotyonok*. I have to punish you for what you've done, but I still want you." Warmth crept into his face and voice. "I think we will do well together."

Dani considered her options. She could surrender and hope Vladimir didn't kill her, or she could try to shoot her way out. This wasn't a video game, and the stakes were her life. Did she have the courage to fight?

She looked at Vladimir, the easy way out. Maybe not easy, but at least she would survive the night. Her gun weighed her arms down and they dropped slightly.

A footstep behind her had her swinging her arms back up into position. She hadn't realized how far they'd dropped.

Boris stepped into her peripheral vision, his gun pointed right at her. "Mr. Rusakov?" his gruff voice called.

"Don't shoot yet," Vladimir answered. "*Kotyonok*?"

She raised her arms again. The gun felt like it was twenty pounds. "Don't call me that," she said.

His eyebrows arched. "But you're exactly like a kitten hissing in the corner, trying to bite the hand that feeds you."

Her lips firmed. She couldn't go back to Vladimir. She wouldn't help him traffic women and sell them into slavery, she'd rather die. A deep breath in. She knew as soon as she pulled the trigger, Boris would kill her.

At least she'd helped the women escape, and if she could take Vladimir with her, then it was worth it.

His easy smile faded, almost as if he heard her thoughts. He looked to Boris and opened his mouth.

Jake leapt from behind a crate, his gun pointed at Boris. "Shoot, Dani."

Even in the depths of this hellish situation, Dani's body jolted with joy. He hadn't left her.

Boris swung his weapon toward Jake, but too late. Jake shot him in the head and he fell backward. Vladimir's eyes widened and he pulled a pistol from behind his back, aiming for Jake.

She pulled the trigger.

Vladimir staggered back, clutching his stomach.

She'd done it. She'd shot him. He dropped his gun and slumped to his knees.

She stalked over to him, still keeping her pistol trained on him, trusting Jake to watch her back.

"*Kotyonok*?" Vladimir said hoarsely. Blood trickled between his fingers.

"I told you not to call me that." She held her gun to his temple. What if he lived and came after her again, or worse, started selling women again? She should finish him off. Her hands shook.

A large, warm hand covered hers and pushed her weapon down. *Jake.* He stood there, calm and steady, a rock in the midst of her tossing storm. "He's finished, Dani. You don't need to do this."

She stared into his gray eyes and nodded, lowering her gun. "I thought you'd left."

He frowned. A muscle jumped in his jaw. "You thought I'd leave you behind?"

Her mouth opened. Now that he said it like that, she realized Jake had way too much integrity to ever leave anyone behind.

She shook her head and then shrugged. Too many emotions swirled in her.

The thumping sound of a helicopter coming close to the barn made them both raise their heads.

"We'll talk later," Jake said. He checked the rounds in his magazine. "Time to go."

Rapid gunfire outside made them tense.

Vladimir gurgled a laugh from where he kneeled near them. Blood soaked his hands and shirt and pooled around him. "I called for reinforcements. You'll both be dead soon."

Jake cursed and grabbed her hand. They ran to the wide-open front of the barn where they could see what was happening outside.

A helicopter landed in one of the fields just beyond the main house. Muzzle flashes sparked from a machine gun pointing out of one of the open doors. The rapid bark of gunfire ripped through the night. Answering muzzle flashes lit the scene, making everything surreal, as if it were a real war zone.

"I don't get it," Dani panted, preparing her body to run. "Why are they shooting at each other?"

Jake grinned. "Because that's not Vlad's helicopter. The cavalry has finally arrived."

Within a minute, Rhys and Cat showed up, decked out in fatigues, assault rifles in hand. Rhys ducked into the barn with them while Cat crouched in the shadows by the door, her weapon up, scanning for targets.

"It's good to see you, College," Rhys said, gripping Jake's shoulder before nodding at Dani. "And you too, chère. Sorry we're late." He handed Jake a pistol and an extra magazine.

"Where the hell have you been?" Jake said.

Rhys shrugged. "Long story, man. They must have suspected you being at Dani's place was a trap. They had three cars set up, just like the one they'd shoved you into. We got duped in a bad way." He jerked his chin at the door. "It's thanks to Cat we're here at all. She immediately got on the horn with the local police. With her help, they found and tracked your car out to this area. Then it was just a matter of circling our bird until the infrared lit up."

"How'd you know it would light up?" Dani asked.

Rhys grinned. "I've known this guy a long time. There's

no way he'd be able to get out of here without a firefight of some sort."

Jake grunted. "Plan?"

"Hold tight," Rhys said. "Backup is coming." He scanned the bodies sprawled throughout the barn. "Though it looks like you guys have it covered."

CHAPTER 22

D ani sat in the war room with the rest of the
team, staring at her hands gripped in her lap,
knowing the others watched her, their gazes
almost a physical weight.

Knight and Blackwell stood at the front of the room.

"I'm sorry, Dani," Blackwell said. "But—"

Dani stood up. "Wait," she said. "I need to say something
first." She looked at the E.D.G.E. team sitting around the
table.

Jake watched her closely from his seat opposite her. He
still had on the ripped black t-shirt, his muscular biceps
tensed as he waited for her to speak. They hadn't had much
of a chance to talk on the way back from the farm. Police
and CSIS had swarmed the area. The E.D.G.E. team had

pulled out as soon as the reporters had shown up.

She wanted badly to work with these people. To be a part of something bigger, to finally do something worthwhile with her life. In order to do that, though, she had to come clean.

"I need to apologize for lying to you all. I did it because I had been running for so long, that hiding was easier for me than admitting the truth. I was ashamed of who I'd been and I never wanted anyone to find out." She took a deep, cleansing breath.

"I want to be a team member, but I know I need to earn your trust first. You know all my secrets now. I have no reason to hide anymore. I want to work at E.D.G.E., and if that means starting in Research again then I'll do it, but I think that would be a waste of my talents. I can—"

"Enough, Danika," Blackwell said, holding up his palm, his face grim. He looked over at Knight, who nodded.

She kept her gaze on Blackwell, whose dark eyes studied her as if looking for weakness. She vowed he wouldn't find any.

He crossed his arms. "I had planned on firing you." Her stomach clenched, but she didn't flinch outwardly.

"But," he continued, "you've shown an impressive amount of ability under pressure, and incredible loyalty to your team member." He nodded at Jake, whose eyes radiated approval when she looked at him. Pleasure curled in her and somehow strengthened her, before she once again focused on Blackwell.

"You are correct. You do have a skillset we could use." Blackwell smiled, which softened the harsh lines of his face. "It's hard to find IT people of your caliber who can handle this type of work. Welcome to the team, Danika."

After the debrief, Jake waited with her at the elevator.

"How's your friend?" he asked.

"She's still in the hospital, but she'll recover. She's strong. And I'll help her through this." Tassia had had a horrifying experience and Dani would make sure she got all the support she needed to live her life again.

"Good." He shifted his feet. "So what are you going to do now?"

"Home. Long shower. Much sleep," she said. Her insides twisted. "You? Are you heading back to San Diego soon?"

Jake nodded. "Rhys and I are due back in two days."

Her stomach fell and she studied her toes. She wanted to ask him to stay. "Will you be deployed immediately when you get back?"

"I'll have a couple of weeks before I leave."

She peeked up at him and found herself caught in his molten gaze. It seared her insides with its intensity. "Oh," she said. Then his words caught up with her. He was being deployed. "So…I probably won't see you again?"

He smiled. "Well, not for a couple of weeks anyway."

She frowned. "I don't understand."

"I've accepted the position Knight offered. I like what

E.D.G.E. does. I'll always be a SEAL, but this might be a new way for me to serve. I'm starting in two weeks." The elevator doors chimed and opened. He stalked toward her, a devious grin on his face, as she backed into the empty compartment. The doors closed and he pressed her against the wall, his chest against hers. His hands came up to cradle her face.

His lips claimed hers in a kiss that scattered her thoughts and sent need ripping through her. She gripped his shoulders, loving the contained strength under her fingers. He nuzzled that spot behind her ear that sent electricity shooting through her.

Breathless though she was, she wanted more from him. "Is that the only reason you took the job?" she asked.

His eyes searched hers and his head gave a little shake. "No. I'm coming back for you, hacker girl. I'll always come for you."

Her heart swelled in her chest and a smile bloomed on her face. Her life had changed an impossible amount in the last two weeks. She'd gone from living in fear to living life to the fullest. She pulled Jake's head down for a kiss. "And I'll never hide again."

AUTHOR'S NOTE

Thank you so much for reading **Edge of Control**.
It means so much to an author to be able to share their stories with others. If you enjoyed mine then I would appreciate it if you would help others enjoy the book too. You can do this by telling a friend, or writing a review on either Amazon or Goodreads.

ABOUT THE AUTHOR

Trish writes about strong, kickass women who don't need to be rescued and the heroic men who fall for them. Before becoming an author Trish spent time as an officer in the Canadian Army and then worked as a physicist. Now, her career includes being a mother and an author. She considers herself to be a geek and a nerd, though knowing the difference really just makes her a dork. Her addiction to reading rivals her addiction to tea. She lives in Calgary, Alberta with her husband, two girls and one house cat that thinks it's a tiger. To find out more about Trish and her books, visit her website.

www.trishloye.com

MORE BOOKS BY TRISH LOYE

E.D.G.E. SECURITY SERIES

Book 1: **Edge of Control**

Book 2: **Edge of Reason**

Book 3: **Edge of Danger**

COMING SOON!

Christmas Novella: **Edge of the Season** (Dec 2015)

Book 4: **Edge of Courage** (Winter 2016)

If you want to stay up to date on my newest releases
then be sure to sign up for my newsletter.
You can find out more about me and my newsletter at
www.trishloye.com.
I also love to hear from readers so please contact me at
trish@trishloye.com.

Keep reading for a sneak peak of

EDGE OF REASON

BY
TRISH LOYE

The second book in the thrilling
E.D.G.E. SECURITY SERIES.

Now Available!

PROLOGUE

SOMEWHERE IN THE HINDU KUSH, AFGHANISTAN.

Petty Officer Rhys "Lucky" Lafayette's legs burned as he raced to the mountaintop with the dead weight of an unconscious man over his shoulder. His lungs labored to gasp in enough air. Fifty yards to the plateau.

He and the rest of his team had just snatched the kidnapped journalist from the Taliban, who now gave chase. Somewhere at the top of the plateau a helicopter was on its way. He hoped.

His two other teammates already lay in wait at the top, their sniper rifles taking out any Taliban getting too close to him, while his best friend stayed at the bottom and also covered his ass. He pushed harder, knowing the longer he took, the longer Lieutenant Jake "College" Harrison was under heavy fire below him.

Sweat dripped into his eyes. Fucking mountains. Give him a flat beach or, hell, even surf torture any day over this scree-covered shit.

He crested the ridge and spotted his teammates Roddy and Scat aiming their rifles downhill. He lowered the haggard man to the ground behind a boulder to protect him from stray bullets, grateful to be rid of the dead weight. "At the top, College," Rhys said into the comm. "Haul ass."

"Wilco."

Rhys dropped to the ground and sighted along his rifle downhill as Jake did a last spray of bullets into the trees, switched out his mags, and sprinted up the slope.

Rhys breathed deep to slow his heart rate. The butt of his FN SCAR Mk 17 dug into his shoulder as he fired round after round into the Taliban assholes chasing Jake.

The thumping of helicopter rotors sounded close behind him, but he didn't look. It was friendly.

"Run faster, College," he said into his mic.

"Roger," came Jake's panting reply. Sure enough, Rhys watched him speed up.

But it wasn't fast enough. Rhys fired again and again.

A large dark-skinned man in unfamiliar fatigues dropped down beside Rhys with an M249 SAW light machine gun, and started strafing the Taliban soldiers who climbed behind Jake.

"Don't hit my guy," Rhys growled.

"Never," the man answered.

"What unit are you guys?" Rhys asked while still firing.

"E.D.G.E." he replied.

"Edge? What the hell is that?"

"The unit saving your asses."

Rhys would have replied but below him, Jake stumbled and clutched his leg. Rhys's chest tightened as Jake went down to one knee. It looked like he'd taken a hit to the thigh.

Rhys didn't even realize he'd gone to a crouched position. "Get up, Jake!" he screamed.

"Dude, where're you going?" the soldier beside him yelled.

Rhys didn't answer. He ran downslope, slipping in the scree, counting on the rest of his team and the new guy to keep him alive.

Jake was moving again—slower than before, but still upslope. It was a testament to his willpower that he kept going at all. Blood drenched his pant leg.

Rhys slid to a stop by Jake and tucked his shoulder under the shorter man's arm. "Come on, College. You're slower than molasses running uphill."

The new soldier had followed Rhys and took Jake's other arm. Together they got him to the top. More men from the new unit lay down covering fire for them. Rhys breathed a sigh of relief when he saw the helicopter sitting just behind the ridge. Jake would need an immediate evac.

Having crested the ridge, they stood in a relative calm on

higher ground, protected from enemy fire by their location and the soldiers firing downhill keeping the Taliban back. A soldier from this Edge unit carried the journalist to the helicopter.

A tall woman strode toward them, shouldering her rifle. Her blazing blue eyes held his attention. "I'm Valkyrie," she said. "The team leader." She waved at the dark-skinned soldier holding Jake's other arm. "Doc's our medic, he'll see to your leg."

Rhys couldn't help but stare at the woman. What was she doing here? She turned to him, her face stone cold. "Do you have a problem, sailor?"

That stopped him. She knew they were SEALs, even without identifying insignia. "No, sir," he said and then corrected himself, feeling like a heel. "I mean, ma'am."

She rolled her eyes and faced Jake again. "My team can handle this from here. Get on the bird."

Jake didn't move, just stared at Valkyrie. "You're a woman."

Rhys snorted. No shit.

Valkyrie's voice took on an uncompromising edge. "I'm a captain, and you're done here, sailor. This is now my mission."

But Jake, stubborn as always, just kept going. "You're not spec ops."

Rhys almost grinned at the sparks of temper in Valkyrie's eyes. Whoever she was, she wasn't backing down from confronting a SEAL.

"No," she said. "We're E.D.G.E. operators. Now get your ass onboard."

She marched off.

Rhys stared after her. "I think I'm in love."

"Edge?" Jake asked the soldier nicknamed Doc.

"E.D.G.E.," he said, as they helped Jake to the waiting helicopter. "Elite Digital and Global Enforcement unit."

"Never heard of it," Jake muttered.

The soldier grinned. "That's the idea."

Rhys knew that secrets lived within secrets in most governments and military units. But it was unusual they hadn't heard even a whisper of this group before. He helped get Jake settled in the MH-60 Black Hawk. Doc knelt beside him and unzipped a medical kit.

The unconscious journalist had already been strapped down and another soldier lifted his eyelids and shone a light in them.

"Thanks for your help, Doc," Rhys said.

"No worries." He applied clotting powder and bandages to Jake's wound, while the other soldier on board turned and immediately got a tourniquet wrapped around Jake's upper thigh, before pulling a saline drip out of a medical kit.

"We'll take care of your friend," Doc said.

An explosion thundered on the slope behind them. Rhys hoped that these E.D.G.E. guys had set that off and not the tangos.

Doc touched his PTT button on his headset and spoke

into the mic. "Roger, Valkyrie." Then he nodded at Rhys. "She needs another set of hands outside."

"I'm on it." Rhys jumped out of the helicopter. Valkyrie crouched behind a boulder with two other men. Gunfire had escalated in the area. He raced over to them and hunkered down.

"We need to get out of here," he said.

She scowled at him. "The Taliban just got reinforcements."

"Let me guess. They've got RPGs." Rocket-propelled grenades could shoot their helicopter out of the sky.

She nodded. "But don't worry, I've got something better." She pulled out six small metal balls from one of the pouches on her webbing.

"You gonna play marbles?" Rhys asked.

She handed three to one of the soldiers and then pointed down one side of the slope in front of them. "Position them there."

"Wilco," the guy said, and he and his buddy took off, staying low.

She watched them for a moment. "Okay. Cover me while I set these little guys."

Valkyrie took off—Rhys had no choice but to follow her. She ran down the mountain straight toward the tangos.

"Are you fucking crazy?" Rhys yelled.

She slid to a stop next to another boulder and crouched behind it. "We can't let the tangos hide in these rocks. They'll be able to take down our bird with those RPGs before we reach altitude." She pulled a strip of plastic off the back of one and stuck it to the rock face in the direction of the tangos.

"What are those things?" Rhys asked.

"Motion-sensor explosives. I designed them myself," she said with a grin.

He wanted to grin back, but this was serious stuff. "But will they work?" She scowled at him. "I just meant they're kinda tiny."

"It's not the size that matters," she said. Her lips quirked in a small smile. "I'm sure you've heard that before. Now cover me."

Before Rhys could think of a reply, she started setting her charges and he went to work firing at any tangos that popped their heads out of the woods below.

As soon as they left, the tangos would rush this slope and land right in the motion sensor's path. He prayed this woman knew what she was doing. He wasn't sure he fully trusted her yet, but she seemed confident about her little bombs.

"They're coming closer," he said. "You done yet?"

"Almost." She moved further downslope to another set of rocks, closer to the tangos.

"Woman, you are driving me insane," he muttered as he followed her, firing as he went.

She hunched down and set the last explosive. A bullet pinged off the rock near her head. Rhys waited for a reaction, but she didn't flinch, just continued working with steady hands. He picked off the tango who'd gotten too close.

"Done. Let's move, sailor," she said. She grabbed her rifle and laid down covering fire. "Run!" she barked at him.

He scowled. "I'm not leaving you."

She looked at him like he was crazy. "Of course you're not. But you must be almost out. Change your mag while you're on the move and then cover me."

"No way," he said, changing his mag while he crouched beside her behind the boulder. "We go together."

Her eyes blazed with anger. She shot more rounds at the encroaching enemy, swore, and then ran up the mountain.

He sprayed another burst and then followed her, pumping his legs, expecting to catch her within a few steps. He planned to run right behind her to protect her back with his body.

But he never got the chance. She raced up the mountain like some kind of deer. He pushed hard, not wanting to be hit by the gunfire that followed them, and he gained on her, but he didn't catch her.

He made the top and ducked behind the ridge, laying flat out beside her to watch the tangos enter their trap.

"Three little bombs might not be enough," he said. "Why don't you get on the bird? My guys and I can cover you and then haul ass to the next ridge where you can circle back for us."

"Shut the fuck up," she said.

"Listen, woman—"

She turned to him. "Call me Valkyrie, or don't call me

anything. Now stay on target." She watched down the mountain. The tangos started running full bore up toward them.

Rhys swore to himself. There were too many of them. If they didn't get out of here they'd be slaughtered. He signaled his two other teammates to fall back to the helicopter.

He grit his teeth. He would get this woman, this Valkyrie, out of here even if he had to throw her over his shoulder and carry her to the helicopter. He'd started to rise when she grabbed his shoulder and hauled him back down.

"Three, two, one," she said.

The tangos had crossed into whatever kill zone she'd set up. The explosion boomed across the valley, followed by two more in quick succession. Pulverized rocks and dust covered the area, making it impossible to see.

A vibrating rumble shook the ground under them. The dust began to clear, and he saw Taliban soldiers bracing themselves where they stood or had fallen.

A deafening crack stopped the vibrations. A new mushroom cloud of dust surged up and over the area. At the same time, the thunderous crashing of rocks slid down the mountain in an avalanche, the men screaming as they fell under the wave of it.

"Shit," Rhys breathed. "Remind me never to piss you off."

She stood up and walked over to the waiting helicopter without replying.

Now *that* was a woman. Rhys grinned.

On the bird flying back to safety, she pretended to ignore

him, but he could see her glancing at him from the corner of her eye every once in a while.

This wasn't over.

He would find out what E.D.G.E. was, because he planned to meet Valkyrie again.

51950633R00181

Made in the USA
Charleston, SC
07 February 2016